DAYRAVEN

HYGELAC'S RAID

SWORD OF WODEN

C.R.MAY

This novel is a work of fiction. The names, characters and incidents portrayed in it, while at times based on real figures, are purely the work of the author's imagination.It is sold subject to the condition that it shall not by way of trade or otherwise, be lent, resold, hired out, or otherwise circulated without the writer's prior consent, electronically or in any form of binding or cover other than the form in which it is published and without a similar condition including this condition being imposed on the subsequent purchaser. Replication or distribution of any part is strictly prohibited without the written permission of the copyright holder.

Dayraven

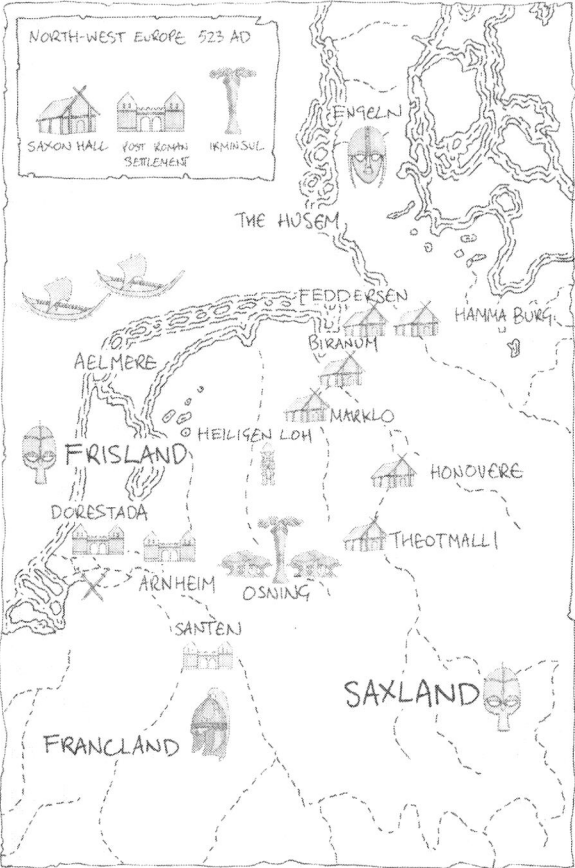

NORTH-WEST EUROPE 523 AD

SAXON HALL POST ROMAN SETTLEMENT IRMINSUL

ENGELN

THE HUSEM

FEDDERSEN

HAMMA BURG

BIRANUM

AELMERE

MARKLO

HEILIGEN LOH

HONOVERE

FRISLAND

THEOTMALLI

DORESTADA

OSNING

ARNHEIM

SANTEN

SAXLAND

FRANCLAND

... attacked the Francish lands over the deep sea with a ship borne host. They laid waste a district belonging to Theodoric, that of the Hetware or others, and carried off captives; then they went aboard their ships, which were full of captives, setting out for the deep sea, with their king remaining on the sea shore. When this news had been brought to Theodoric he sent his son Theudobert to those parts with a large army...

Liber Historiae Francorum

ONE

The scouts slipped noiselessly from their saddles and hurried across to the old man who was beckoning to them from the shadow of the doorway. The young boy ran before them and his grandfather tousled his hair affectionately as he ushered him inside. Placing a gnarled finger to his lips he indicated that the warriors follow him with a flick of his head and, stooping low, he led them along the side of the ramshackle hut and pointed to a small hall at the eastern edge of the village.

The leader patted the old man on the shoulder, slipping him a silver coin as the warriors' swords slid free from their scabbards and they awaited his signal to attack. At least he and the boy would eat for a while, and besides, loyalty *should* be rewarded. Beyond the ragged line of trees to the east the iron-grey light of the pre dawn was finally retreating before the first splash of pinks and reds as the sun broke free of the worlds rim. Glancing back towards the roadway they watched two shadowy figures scurried along the edge of the settlement, and they exchanged nervous smiles when the men froze as the raucous call of a cockerel welcomed the dawn of a new day.

The Franc cursed silently, the bird could do for them all. The boy had told him that there were only six of the enemy in the settlement, but he had learned the hard way that his own eyes were far better at judging enemy numbers than six or seven year old lads. He paused as he weighed up the choices open to him. Even if the boy had underestimated their number he had thirteen experienced warriors in his patrol. There was only one action open to him he knew. He must attack or appear cowardly, and the Lord in Heaven knew that the people in this area had suffered enough at the hands of the barbarians already that summer. The cockerel crowed again and he decided to skirt the clearing ahead, hugging the cover which the large woodpile there would afford them. It would delay the attack for a few moments but that could not be helped.

Kari groaned and slowly opened one eye as the boot playfully kicked his foot again.

"Come on, wake up big nose!"

The dream horses had carried him back to the arms of his family for a brief time, and although he enjoyed his life on campaign, the nights without them around him were the hardest.

"Kari, let's get going, you know that it is your turn!"

He rolled on his back and threw off his cloak in resignation, smiling up at the face of his friend. Today would be the last day of scouting duties, if nothing of note appeared ahead of them by the middle of the day they would start heading back to the main army. They crisscrossed the road which led as straight as any spear shaft south into the heart of the kingdom of the Francs for several days now, and had discovered nothing more threatening to the great Geatish ship army they had left at the river than a few ceorls and their cows. These people were soft, he decided, no wonder that the king had chosen them to raid.

It had been almost two months since they had fallen on the northern provinces of the Fris and routed their army. Scouring the land they had marched south, shadowed by the ships of the fleet, and crossed the great inland sea of the Aelmere. Moving on into the great river system of the Vecht and Rin, they had laughed and joked happily as the forces of the Fris and Francs had fled before them like deer before a wildfire. Soon the raid would be over and they could regain the ships and sail back to their northern homes in triumph, rich beyond their dreams. He would extend the farm and invest in more cattle. Scouting was good, it offered untold opportunities to unearth hastily hidden riches in the unguarded farms and settlements. His family were about to move up in the world, he reflected happily. His daughter was almost seven winters old now and thoughts were beginning to turn to marriage. Now that his standing in the community was about to increase they could set their sights higher than the local boys. If the gods were willing, the son of a thegn was coming within reach for them. Such a kinship connection would see the fortunes of his family surge to new heights. Maybe his baby son could be fostered at the hall of this lucky thegn he speculated cheerfully as a monotone grunt broke into his thoughts.

"Food!"

Kari glanced across and smiled at the big man who still lay tightly cocooned in his cloak on the opposite side of the hearth. Thorvald was always hungry but his strength and appetite were allied to an amiable nature which made him a popular leader of the group. Kari winked at him, and was rewarded with a wide smile as he rose from the straw strewn floor of the hut and made his way over to the bag of food which the scavenging of previous few days had provided for them. Scooping up his weapons he sheathed his sword and, with a last glance at his four slumbering companions, ducked out into the sultry morning air. It was barely a week since the midsummer solstice and the nights were short, already the sun was gilding the eastern horizon and a cockerel dutifully crowed on the far side of the small settlement. Kari chuckled to himself as he sleepily dragged his protesting body alongside the hut towards the place where they had hobbled their horses.

It's a good thing that he kept quiet last night or he would have been in the pot!

As he neared the corner of the building a series of soft, muffled sounds carried to him and his mind snapped back from its meanderings. Instinctively he pressed himself back against the wall and listened intently. The unmistakable sounds made by scuffling men were coming from the direction of the horse line. Carefully dropping the food Kari slowly drew his sword, grimacing as the blade slid from the mouth of the scabbard with its familiar swish. Harald, he knew was there alone and would need help quickly if he was under attack. As Kari made to dart forward from the shadows, a movement to his right caught his eye and he froze instantly. Slowly turning his head he was horrified to see armed men, warriors, ducking into the hut which he had left moments before. A heartbeat later the air was filled by the last confused cries of his companions as they were slaughtered where they lay.

His mind raced. The men in the hut were clearly beyond help and Harald had almost certainly joined them on the rainbow bridge which led to valhall by now. He must be the last survivor of their little band and his duty was clear. The men he had seen were high class warriors, tough looking and well armed. This was no attack by the forces of the local thegn, an army must be approaching from the South. He must get the news back to the king.

Already, curious faces were beginning to peer from the doorways of the settlement. In a few moments they would realise what was happening and reveal his presence to their own warriors, he must move now. Steeling himself Kari burst from cover and raced across the small track which served the settlement as a main thoroughfare. Rounding the final hut, he broke out into the clearing beside the old Roman Road which bounded the place. Before him two of the enemy warriors were bent over the body of his friend Harald, roughly searching his blood-soaked body for any items of value.

Fighting against the urge to scream a battle cry Kari tore across towards the men, twisting his body as he drew back his sword for a killing stroke. At the last moment the warrior on the far side glanced up, and Kari almost laughed as the man's cheerful expression changed in a heartbeat to one of shock and horror as he recognised his death bearing down upon him.

Kari leapt onto the back of the nearest Franc, unwinding all the power in his body as he did so. His sword flashed down as he channelled all of his strength into the killing strike. The furthest warrior managed to throw up his arm in a pathetic attempt at deflecting the blow but Kari's blade severed the limb and keened on into the head beyond. Cries of alarm were beginning to carry to him from the settlement now and he knew that the inhabitants were trying to attract the attention of their lord's men to the danger at the horse line. The Franc had still been wearing his helm and the resistance it had offered had caused his blade to remain wedged tightly in the man's head. The second Franc was beginning to recover from his surprise and scramble to his feet. Kari knew that he had to act quickly or he would die here.

Releasing the grip on his sword he flicked up the strap which held his short seax in its scabbard and tore the weapon free. Throwing himself on the back of the warrior, Kari plunged the seax into the man's exposed neck, sawing the wicked blade as great gouts of arterial blood pumped out to soak the dusty ground.

Quickly clambering to his feet the Geat scout shot a panic-stricken glance back towards the huts as he wrestled the sword blade clear of his *fiend's* helm. A knot of women had gathered on the central track which led through the settlement and they were pointing and crying out in their strange tongue. The Geat knew that he had moments left in which to make his escape before the friends of the men he had slain would arrive, and he was under no illusions as to the likelihood of his surviving such a meeting.

Scampering across, Kari feverishly untied the leather bindings which were hobbling his mount and vaulted into the saddle. Big Thorvald, the leader of the group, had insisted that they replace the saddles once the horses had been groomed the previous evening, despite the tired men's protests, and Kari gave thanks as he now recognised that his leader's foresight had at least given him a chance to escape with his life.

The king's army was encamped barely fifteen miles to the North and he would be back and safely within its ranks inside the hour. All he had to do was regain the Roman Road which bounded the settlement and ride like the wind, directly back to them.

Kari wheeled his horse and glanced back just as the leading Francish warriors hove into view.

Too late my friends!

Reassured, he turned back to the roadway but stared in horror at the sight which greeted him. Only feet before him a boy was running, grim faced, towards him, his arms preparing to thrust an ancient spear into his belly. Quickly he twisted his body and slipped sideways in a desperate attempt to deflect the blow but the gods had finally deserted him. Thrust forward from such a low angle the shaft of the spear slid along the inside of Kari's thigh and carried on. His instinctive reaction to avoid the attack had provided just enough space for the boy's pathetic weapon to burrow in under the lower edge of his mail shirt. Kari gasped in shock and pain as the point of the spear slid easily into his unprotected groin and he spurred his horse towards the boy who fell back in terror. Kari gritted his teeth against the pain and tugged the spear from his body with a horrible sucking sound. Spinning it expertly in his hand, he drew his arm back to skewer the boy who had wounded him. A scream came from a nearby hut and he glanced across to see what was obviously the boy's mother silhouetted in the doorway, her features contorted in horror. The boy still stood, transfixed and defenceless, before him but the mother's cry had saved her son's life. He swept the point of the spear across and struck the boy a glancing blow on the side of the head, throwing the weapon away in disgust. He would have a scar to remind him of the day that he wounded the barbarian and saved the settlement, but he would live.

The sound of horse bits jangling brought his mind crashing back into focus and, kicking in, he thundered back down the road. Leaning forward close to his mount's neck Kari flew north. He risked a backward glance and was gratified to see that the leading members of the chasing pack were at least a hundred yards behind him, frantically urging on their mounts as they gained the roadway, their great blue cloaks billowing in their wake.

The sun was just clearing the tree line to his right, its golden light throwing a latticework of shadows across the ancient paving and he began to relax and take stock of his situation as the horse settled into a steady rhythm. Another quick glance behind confirmed that the Francs were not gaining on him, in fact, he noted with relief, they seemed to be slowly losing ground. That made sense he reflected. His horse had eaten and drunk well and was fresh from a night's rest whereas those of his pursuers must have ridden through the night to get here at dawn. They would be tired and hungry, and now they were being asked to race fifteen miles against a fresh mount. Kari had specifically looked to see if they had thought to bring his dead companions' horses along as remounts, but it would seem that they had neglected to do so in their haste. He started to relax. Nothing could now stop him from regaining the Geatish army at the river. Once there he would have his wound looked at by one of the cunning women which had accompanied the ship army for just that purpose. He may even let one of the 'crows' they had taken for thraldom see what he could do. The black kirtled wizards of the Roman nailed god all seemed to possess some knowledge of such things. He remembered men discussing how it would increase the price they would fetch at the slave market in Nyen. Even the pain in his groin seemed to be lessening he noted with satisfaction.

He moved his hand down to gently massage the area and flicked a look dawn at his palm.

Shit!

He blanched as he saw that his hand was covered in thick, dark blood. Craning forward, he ran his palm along the side of his saddle and slowly down the flanks of his horse. To his consternation all felt warm, wet and sticky and he realised to his horror that he was now in a race against time. Ahead of him a stone bridge led across one of the interminable rivers which seemed to snake their way across the landscape. His horse shot from the cover of the tree line and clattered across as it continued its remorseless journey north.

Kari closed his eyes and soaked up the welcome warmth of the early morning sun which now fell directly upon him. He had not realised until then just how chilled he had become as the ride progressed, and he realised with a start that he was beginning to succumb to the effects of blood loss. He had seen enough men die in the last few months to recognise the symptoms and he desperately packed his groin with his cloak in an effort to staunch the flow, but the realisation that this sunrise would be his last was now breaking upon him.

His thoughts began to swim as he dimly realised that his horse was slowing. Desperately shaking his head to try and clear his thoughts, Kari found to his surprise that he was leaning back and facing the sky. He began to feel dizzy and nauseous as a brace of swans, huge and startlingly white against the soft blue-grey sky, swept across his line of sight and his head lolled in their direction of flight. To his left a wide flower strewn water meadow opened out running down to a small copse of alder, and he smiled as he recognised that it almost exactly mirrored the southern boundary of his own farm in far off Geatland. It was a sign he knew, and he hauled on the reins and walked the animal across as the sound of hurrying hoof beats carried to him from the bridge.

Kari felt inside his kirtle and tugged out the small wooden amulet which hung suspended there. He brought the small roughly carved hammer of Thunor to his lips and kissed it tenderly, breathing in softly in an attempt to detect any lingering trace of the hands which had so lovingly carved it. It had been a parting gift from his young daughter at the start of summer and he had worn it proudly ever since, but, to his disappointment, the rigours of the summer campaign had removed all trace of her scent.

He closed his eyes and turned his face towards the warmth of the sun for the last time in this life as he became aware of the hubbub made by bees all around him as they harvested the tapestry of wildflowers. He realised dimly that his breathing had become laboured as his vision began to lose focus and he struggled to stay upright. Final thoughts of home flickered into his mind and he smiled sadly. The local boys would be as good as any thegn's son for young Signy he knew. They were strong and honest, good boys from fine families.

Drawing his sword for the last time, Kari slipped painfully from his mount and waited for the line of grim faced Francs as they advanced slowly across the meadow towards him.

TWO

King Hygelac clapped his hands together and strode across the dock front towards the waiting thegns and ealdormen.

"Don't tell me, porridge and sausage?"

The assembled warriors turned and laughed, grinning widely as their lord approached. Flosi, the king's cook, looked up from his work and smiled a welcome.

"Porridge and Sausage it is, lord. The finest to be had on the River Rin!"

It was porridge and sausage every day and this day would be no different. It was the meal which all of the Geatish army would have to break their fast, from the king himself to the lowliest member if the baggage train. Hygelac made a point of moving among the men and sharing their food and they respected him all the more for it. Flosi dolled out a large helping of the steaming mixture and sent a boy over to the king with it. Nodding his thanks, Hygelac blew on his first spoonful as he regarded his men.

"Anything to report?"

Hromund, ealdorman of Geatwic and one of the king's oldest friends grimaced.

"I have to report that this *laager* that they drink down here makes me feel like shit in the morning lord. Have we got any good Geatish ale left?"

Hygelac chuckled.

"I suggest that you don't try to drink it all yourself and leave some for us then!"

The group laughed as Hygelac continued.

"What about those missing scouts, have they turned up yet?"

Hromund shook his head, wincing as he did so.

"No, lord, I imagine that they are struggling to carry back all their booty. I sent out a party just before dawn to see if they could find them. They have orders to ride south until the sun climbs to its high point and return. If they are still unaccounted for I suggest that we start to make our way to the coast without them."

The king nodded thoughtfully.

"Start to break camp now, we'll move downriver this morning. I don't want to linger here any longer now that we have split the army."

They were in the place which the Fris called Dorestada, right on the southern border of their lands. The Geatish ship army had used the place as a secure base from which to send out raiding parties both by land and along the great river systems which meandered their way across the endless flatlands hereabouts, the Rin, the Masa, the Woh and the Sceald. Laying on the northern bank of the mighty River Rin, the town offered endless opportunities to sally forth against the rich towns and settlements of the Salian Francs which lay to the South.

Hygelac reflected on the success of his raid that summer as he stood and gazed across the flatlands. They had sailed south at the beginning of the summer and fallen on the Hugas, one of the tribes which comprised the Fris, before they had even known that they were coming. Laying waste the land they had surprised the main Frisian army at its muster and destroyed it piecemeal. He had detached his foster son Beowulf with gifts for the Saxon king, Gewis, and a promise to respect their borders which ran along the Rivers Emesa and Rin to safeguard his left flank and marched south.

Half of the army had crossed the great inland sea of the Aelmere and come to Dorestada via the Vecht and Rin, capturing the port for use as a base for raiding further south whilst the remainder skirted the eastern shore, plundering as they went. Once the forces had reunited at Dorestada it had been the turn of the ship army to ravage the fat towns of the Hetware and Bructeri to the South whilst the remainder of the army fortified their base against any reprisals by their overlord, the Francish king, Theodoric. To their satisfaction no avenging army had materialised and the Geats were now keen to be away. Several days previously Hygelac had dispatched the majority of the ships downstream loaded with the captives and treasure which had resulted from the campaign under the leadership of his son, Heardred. The remainder of the army would leave Dorestada and make a final foray along the bank of the Rin to its mouth where they would board the ships for home.

Hygelac tipped his bowl and scooped out the last scrapings of porridge. The raid had succeeded beyond his wildest dreams. Losses had been light and his reputation will have soared, both at home and abroad. *Hygelac the Great* he snorted. It sounded good, he could easily get used to it.

A voice sounded at his shoulder, it was Hromund.

"Heardred was right."

Hygelac glanced at his friend.

"In what way?"

Hromund indicated the land to the South, across the massive stone bridge.

"It *is* as flat as a *wicce's* tit!"

Hygelac laughed again at his son's description of the land of the Frisians as he plopped his empty bowl on top of his friends.

"He should know. The appetite for women that boy has never ceases to amaze me."

Hromund smiled at his king's comment but continued to gaze south as movement on the road caught his eye.

"Something is wrong, lord." He murmured.

Hygelac looked back and shielded his eyes as he squinted into the early morning sun. A knot of riders had appeared on the road south where it skirted the small wood. An offshoot of the main river crossed the road there he knew and the locals had banked its course in an effort to keep it from continually flooding. The action had produced what must be regarded as a ridge in these parts and he had always marked it out as a possible forward position for a defence of the town if the need arose. He counted the riders. Two, maybe three, it was difficult to tell at this distance, but they were moving fast, bent forward, their cloaks rippling in their wake.

Hygelac and Hromund instinctively moved towards the northern entrance to the stone bridge to intercept the riders. The guards there moved aside as the king and his ealdorman waited impatiently for the scouts to arrive. The riders reached the southern entrance to the bridge and began to curb their mounts. They were becoming used to riding on paved roads but there was still a reluctance in the army of the Geats to trust the horses to come to a halt on the unfamiliar surface. It was, they all agreed, akin to riding on ice. The scouts picked out the figure of their king and rode towards him. Reining in the leading rider slipped from his saddle and nodded in supplication.

"Lord. The army of the Francs is moving against us along this road."

Hygelac placed his hand on the man's shoulder and nodded that he understood but held up a finger to delay the rider's report. Turning, he called across to the guard commander.

"Hjalti, can you find a drink for these men? They have ridden hard to bring us important news and I think that they would appreciate it." The king indicated a large box which stood beside the parapet. "The ale that you hide under that box would do," he smiled.

Hjalti nodded and smiled sheepishly. Drinking ale on guard duty was forbidden on campaign but most good commanders turned a blind eye if the men remained alert. He threw back the box and filled three cups with ale, hurrying across to hand one to each of the scouts. The rider closed his eyes as he drank, savouring the ale as it refreshed his parched throat. The morning was warm and they had ridden hard, the drink had been more than welcome.

Hygelac waited until the man had drained the cup and smiled encouragingly. It was important to the men that he was seen to remain calm, however bad the news that these scouts were bringing. The men would spot any sign of panic or lack of composure on the part of their leaders and the news would spread through the army like wildfire. In their already reduced numbers the effects could lead to a catastrophe.

The scout nodded his thanks to his king and, clearing his throat, made to make his report but Hygelac held up a hand to stop him.

"Do you know my name?" he asked.

The scout looked confused and blurted out; "yes lord, you are my king, Hygelac Swerting."

Hygelac smiled warmly.

"Then you have your king at a disadvantage because I am afraid that I don't know yours young man."

The man smiled and pulled himself proudly upright.

"My name is Einar Haraldson and these men are Oslaf and Offa, lord."

Hygelac looked across and nodded.

"Oslaf and Offa, Engles?"

"Yes, lord!" they beamed.

"A fine people," Hygelac replied. "My grandson, Weohstan, is an Engle."

He turned back to the scout leader.

"So, Einar Haraldson, what more can you tell me about these Francs?"

"Lord. The army of the Francs is travelling up this road towards us here. I estimate that the first scouting elements will be here shortly with the full army arriving..." he paused and bit his bottom lip as he thought. "Certainly within the hour, lord, we made contact with their scouts on the road and their survivors would have reported back to the main column that we escaped them."

Hygelac raised an eyebrow in surprise.

"They had survivors?"

The warrior looked apologetic and a little shamefaced as he replied.

"I am afraid so, lord. Two of their riders detached themselves from the rear of the column and raced back down the road before we even reached them."

Hygelac nodded thoughtfully as he listened to the scouts report. His mind was already beginning to weigh the advantages and disadvantages of the various options which were still open to him. He now knew the time and place of any clash between the opposing forces, he just needed the final, all important piece of information.

"Did you see the Francish army?"

Einar nodded.

"After we had killed the remaining scouts I climbed a tree and looked back along the road. As you know lord the land here is a flat as..." he paused as he sought an apt description for his king. Hygelac saved him the trouble.

"A *wicce's* tit?"

" A *wicce's* tit, lord," he agreed with a grin before continuing.

"From the top of the tree I could see what must have been a good part of their army before the dust obscured them. I would estimate that I could see at least ten thousand of the fiend, lord."

Hygelac and Hromund shared a look of horror.

"Ten thousand!"

The scout nodded sombrely.

"I am certain of it, lord. We will be facing at least that number. The gods only know how far back the column stretched."

Hygelac nodded as he thought.

At least ten thousand, it could be twenty thousand!

He quickly came to the only decision that was possible under the circumstances. They would have to fight a holding action if they were to have any chance of escape. They could not hope to outrun such numbers all the way to the coast *and* still have time to go aboard the ships. Besides, he snorted, he had never run from an enemy before and he was not going to start now!

Hygelac glanced around the warriors on the bridge. They were all looking his way, counting on him to give them a chance and he must not let them down. He grinned cheerfully at them and called across to the thegn charged with guarding the bridge.

"Hjalti…"

"Yes, lord?"

"How wide would you say that this bridge is?"

Hjalti's lips puckered as he calculated the width.

"Twenty paces, lord?" he ventured.

Hygelac nodded.

"That is about what I make it too."

He turned back to Einar and his English companions.

"I take it that this fiend were not carrying boats?"

"No, lord."

"In that case," Hygelac grinned happily, "unless they can fly the whole of Francland can march on us because we hold the bridges!"

*

Dayraven poked in the ashes with his boot. He knew that it *must* be hereabouts and he would find it if it took him the rest of the day. Suddenly a voice exclaimed excitedly from a little further along the fire eaten stumps of the hall posts.

"Here, lord. I think I have it!"

The warrior hastened across and handed the palm sized metal object to him. Dayraven cradled the spear point in his hand and gently smeared away the sooty residue from the blade with his thumb.

"Here, lord. Try this."

His man had magically produced a small pail of water from somewhere and Dayraven smiled his thanks. He swished the ancient blade gently from side to side, watching in delight as the layers of soot and ash floated free to stain the water, slowly revealing the finely inlaid bronze swirls and patterns which had so captivated him as a boy. The spear blade had not only been one of his father's most treasured possessions, but of *his* father before that, back through countless generations. The thought that it may have been taken by the pirate army had caused the big Frisian to feel sick to his stomach. To his relief it would appear that they had missed this small treasure as they had ransacked his childhood home. Perhaps defiling his sister and burning his mother from her hall had satiated their greed for that day. He held the small blade up and was rewarded with a smile from his mother, the first that he had seen since his return to this ravaged land.

Barely one week ago his world had seemed to be an ordered and happy place. Dayraven had been riding the boundary of his estate overlooking the River Aeldu in the lands which were coming to be known as Anglia, discussing the forthcoming betrothal of his young daughter to the son of his neighbour and friend, Saimund. Neither he nor his hall reeve had taken much notice of the dracca which was approaching the settlement the local Engles called Snæp until he had recognised the sea eagle flag of Frisland snapping at its masthead. Riding down to the riverside he had discovered to his horror that a northern ship army had descended on his homeland and were sweeping with fire and sword through his ancestral lands.

It would seem that the inexperienced young Frisian king, Ida, had panicked and ordered the army of the Fris to muster at the traditional meeting place, known to all as the hoary apple tree, despite the fact that it was close to the marauding pirate army. The inevitable had happened and the thegns and ealdormen of Frisland had been routed one by one as they made their way to the muster. Although several of the ealdormen and more experienced thegns had managed to extricate themselves and retain the bulk of the army intact they had been in no position to organise an effective defence and the pirates had roamed the land at will.

Dayraven had quickly sent word to the men who owed him service to meet at his hall in Fris tun. He had ridden over to Saimund's ham to explain that he would be unable to attend the betrothal and been rewarded with the gift of a fully fitted out and crewed dracca by his English friend. Word had spread fast and another ship had been sent to aid him by the English lord in nearby Rendil's ham.

Within the week they had sailed and two days later he was standing in what remained of his family hall.

Dayraven, hero of the Frisians, had returned in their hour of need with vengeance in his heart.

THREE

Hygelac clattered to the top of the small rise and reined in, peering anxiously south as his warriors fanned out to either side. He was a little disappointed but unsurprised to see that the Francish column was already in sight on the horizon and looming larger with every passing moment but at least he had gained the embankment before the enemy scouts could seize what must pass for the heights in these parts. He snorted happily as he saw the closest group of enemy riders pull on their reins and mill about in confusion as they noticed the Geats appear on the embankment only half a mile before them and hastily deploy into their shield wall. It had been a close run thing and Hygelac hoped that it bode well for the remainder of the day.

As soon as Einar had finished his report Hygelac had sent runners throughout the town with orders to roust every remaining warrior and tell them to head straight for the southern bridge. He had entrusted his ealdorman and friend, Hromund, with the task of destroying as much of the bridge as possible. The king had left five hundred warriors of their much reduced army to help the ealdorman's men weaken the bridge by channelling out the lime mortar which bound the stone together. At the same time men were sent to the dock area to find boats small enough to wedge tightly beneath the arches. Once in place these would be filled with flammable material and placed under guard as word was sent forward to the king and his men that all was ready. In a lull between attacks the Geats would mount up and race back across to the northern bank of the Rin. Once across the boats would be fired and the bridge should collapse very soon in its weakened state. Now separated from the huge Francish army by the River Rin the Geats would carry on to the coast and board the fleet as planned.

With every passing moment more and more Geat warriors were arriving on the embankment and rushing forward to take up their positions alongside the king. Hygelac cast an appreciative look to either side of his defensive position. The Geat shield wall already spanned the roadway and its adjacent land and the wall was growing ever thicker with every passing moment.

Fifty paces to his left the line had anchored itself against a small wood which grew hard onto the river bank. To his right the ground fell away in a gentle slope and the Frisian builders had obviously decided to let the flood waters keep possession of the low marshy ground there once the threat to the roadway had been removed by the gradient of the grassy slope. It would be, in truth, more river than land Hygelac suspected during the wetter months but even at the height of summer he was content that no threat would be likely to materialise from that direction.

Immediately before them a shorter version of the stone bridge at Dorestada spanned the steeply banked stream and it was here that Hygelac had raised the white boar banner of Geatland surrounded by the warriors of his personal comitatus. It was, he noted with satisfaction, an outstanding defensive position. It was so good in fact that he suspected that he recognised the hand of the Allfather in its provision and he sent a silent promise to the god that he would sacrifice his finest war stallion in thanks once they had safely escaped the avenging Francs.

Hygelac watched as the leading horsemen of the Francish army shook themselves free of the tree cover and came on, straight down the road which led to their position. Resplendent in highly polished scale armour, the leading warriors drew to a halt one hundred paces ahead of the Geat war flag, their *herebeacn*, as riders bearing the emblems of the tribes of the Francish peoples moved forward to enclose them in a crescent of brilliant colour. To their rear a seemingly never ending column of armoured warriors spewed forth from the shadows and uncurled themselves, serpent-like, across the face of the water meadow. It was, Hygelac had to admit, a breathtaking display of martial prowess.

A freshening wind had sprung up from the West, driving away the earlier clamminess, and the flags and long tailed *draco* of the Francs curled and snapped out their defiance at the watching Geats. High above, serried ranks of ragged dark clouds dashed on eastwards and a low mournful howl came from the polished heads of the Francish draco as the breeze searched out gaping mouths.

Hygelac leaned across to his hearth warrior, Thurgar, and winked.

"I love those draco. I think that we should mount one as a trophy back of Gefrin. It is time to offer a little incentive to the boys."

Stepping out Hygelac smiled and walked confidently along the face of the Geat line. The warriors turned to face him one by one as word spread among them that their king was about to address the shield wall.

"Aren't they pretty!" he cried as he swept his arm to the South; "It is obvious now why they waited the whole summer before they managed to summon up the courage to face our little raid," he grinned, "they were waiting for their women to finish making the pretty flags!" A murmur of laughter came from the ranks as he continued. "I especially like those draco of theirs. For those of you who are unsure which ones I mean they are the brass dragon heads with the long flowing silk tails. I especially like the way that they howl as the wind passes through them," he paused to smirk mischievously along the shield wall, "they remind me of the *Cwen,* my lovely wife," he grinned as a rumble of laughter rolled along the line. "In fact," he cried, "I like them so much that I am willing to offer a hoard to the man who can bring one of those draco safely to my hall at Gefrin." Hygelac unfastened his helm and removed it. Tossing it high into the air he snatched it back as it fell and held it high. "Now I am sure that many of you think that the king has a big head," he smiled, "and today you could be thankful for it." Hygelac could see that the men were intrigued now as an excited chatter began to pass along the line and he cried out to ensure that every man heard his offer. "The man who brings me that gift will receive payment in gold, enough to fill this helm to the brim!" Astonished gasps left the mouths of the Geat warriors. For many of them the king was offering to pay more than a man could expect to accomplish from a lifetime of toil.

Hygelac replaced his helm and addressed the animated shield wall.

"They look great in number these Francs but they are not Geats!" he cried.

Hygelac picked out the leader of the scouts from earlier that morning to drive his point home.

"Einar Haraldson!"

"Yes, lord!" the man beamed proudly.

"How many men were in this Franc scouting party which you intercepted this morning?"

"Twelve, Lord, two of the riders detached themselves and withdrew before we were able to close with them, so we fought against ten Francish scouts."

Hygelac looked up melodramatically.

"They were hardly confident of victory then?"

Einar grinned and shook his head.

"It would seem not, lord," he agreed.

A distant rumble of thunder rolled across the flatlands from the West as the clouds darkened and swept down on them. Hygelac glanced across and back to the Geat line.

"It would seem that Thunor has come to watch our battle-play today," he smiled. "I will have to double the guard on the ale supplies!" The red bearded god was famous for his feats of eating and ale drinking and the warriors roared with laughter at their king's quip. Hygelac looked back to Einar and continued his interrogation of that morning's clash.

"How many men accompanied you and the English friends I see standing resolutely beside you, Offa and Oslaf , this morning Einar?"

"My kinsman Gunnar Gunnarson, lord, no other."

"He fell?"

"Yes, lord, sword in hand."

Hygelac nodded and lowered his voice in respect for the fallen scout.

"Then he sups in valhall as we speak," he replied sombrely.

Hygelac scanned the battle hardened ranks of Geats arrayed before him and raised his voice once more, ensuring that the facts of the encounter carried to all of the listening warriors.

"Tell us Einar, how many of these Francs survived meeting two Geats and two Engles on the road?"

Einar pulled himself erect as he proudly responded.

"We left none alive, lord!"

The warriors of the Geat shield wall responded with a roar as they acknowledged the bravery and fighting prowess which the scouts had displayed in their victory against such odds. Hygelac smiled to himself and waited for the clamour to abate. All along the line the warriors were beating their spears against shield rims and calling challenges to the silent ranks of the Francish army opposite. Fat drops of rain began to patter the dusty ground around them and Hygelac flicked a look of thanks up to Thunor, the Thunderer. The storm would be a piddling affair but even a misting of damp on top of the grassy meadow would be enough to make an attacker slip and slide. The king judged the moment had come to conclude his battle speech and he turned back to the men.

"Einar and his men proved this morning that each man here is worth at least ten Francish warriors. Thunor has now ensured that they will have to scramble up a greasy slope and scale a muddy bank before they swim across and climb another, even muddier bank, topped by a line of warriors who are so big and ugly that only a mother could love them!" he roared, "and their king of course!" He cried above the answering uproar. Hygelac smiled happily as he strode back across to his position on the bridge to the acclamation of his men. The storm, such as it was, was passing now and the angry black clouds were edged with gold as the sunlight forced its way through. To the West an indigo sky lay marbled with small white clouds promising another fine day.

"That was a generous offer, lord!" Thurgar smiled as Hygelac took back his shield and regained his position beneath the *herebeacn*. Hygelac threw his hearth warrior a wry smile.

"Not really, if I get back to Gefrin it will be a small price to pay. If I don't I shan't have to pay anyway!" he chuckled.

The sound of singing carried up to the Geat position and Hygelac turned back quizzically. A line of men had advanced proud of the Francish front ranks holding aloft flags bearing the mark of the cross as others dressed in the black garb of the Francish priests seemed to be casting protective spells on their warriors. Hygelac turned and called to one of his men as he watched the strange rites.

"Tofi, you talked to the crow-wizards we took. What are they doing down there?"

Tofi called across from his position to the king's right.

"They are singing a type of chant to their god which they call a hymn, lord. The priests are using the wands to flick 'holy water' onto the warriors as a magic charm of protection."

Hygelac shrugged, obviously unimpressed. "Is that so. If I had not just gone I could have flicked some of my own holy water at them," he grinned.

As the men of Hygelac's comitatus laughed at the joke a fire arrow arced into the sky from the right of their position. The king looked across and was surprised to see a small knot of horsemen on the far bank about half a mile downstream. Deliberately placed beyond the line of the embankment they would be able to see both the army of the Francs and the town of Dorestada from their location. He had not noticed them there before and he wondered at their actions. As he did so a section of the army of the Francs gave a great cheer and started to move forward to begin an attack. Hygelac was about to move forward to the far end of the bridge and take up the position of greatest danger and honour when Thurgar caught his arm.

"Lord!"

His battle rage building now the king turned angrily to confront his man and was faced by a breathless and obviously terror stricken warrior he had never seen before. The warrior bowed his head and waited for permission to speak.

"Well, what is it?" Hygelac snapped impatiently.

The warrior swallowed hard and, obviously fighting to retain his composure, replied.

"Lord. Ealdorman Hromund has sent me to report that a large army is moving through the town and is about to engage his forces in Dorstada. He has pulled his warriors together and fallen back on the bridge. He will hold the bridge for as long as he can unless he receives other orders from you."

Hygelac's thoughts swam for a heartbeat as he began to realise that he had been out thought for the first and, it would seem likely, the last time. As the men surrounding him looked on incredulously the king managed to ask the question which was on every man's lips.

"Do we know who this army belongs to?"

The warrior nodded sullenly and replied.

"They fight under the banner of the sea eagle, lord."

Hygelac gasped in disbelief.

"Frisians?"

FOUR

Beowulf gripped the long upward sweep of the stern post and hauled himself up onto the wale. Cupping his hand to his mouth he called across to the figure on the steering platform of the dracca which was breasting the waves to steerboard.

"We will away now, lord. Save some gold for us!"

King Hygelac waved from the deck of his dracca, the *Swan*, and grinning widely, replied to his nephew.

"The gods are with you Beowulf. We will see you in Dorestada after the solstice."

Beowulf took a last look around the Geatish fleet and hauled on the great steer board. The conditions were just right to enable him to leave the other ships with the maximum amount of show. It was childish he knew but great fun just the same.

The Geatish fleet had left their home waters in early summer and, rounding the tip of Jute Land to the West, came about and headed south under a freshening wind. On the morning of the third day at sea the wind had veered around to the north-west and Harald, Hygelac's ship master, had led the fleet out into the German Sea to keep well clear of a lee shore. Beowulf had approved. The ships and crews of the fleet were of varying quality and a group of ships this large would be unwieldy at the best of times. With the wind now blowing directly towards what would be, for most crews, an unfamiliar coast, the margin for any error could vanish with frightening speed. Providing the vast invasion fleet with plenty of sea room was obviously the answer and Beowulf chuckled as he recognised the ships unconsciously begin to huddle closer together for safety as the distant coastline diminished and finally disappeared from view altogether.

The prow of *Wave Dancer* described an arc in the sky ahead and came on to her new heading. With the wind now gusting up from full astern Beowulf ordered the sail fully deployed and sheeted home as the ship filled her great white lung and surged ahead. Her new course would take her straight through the ships of the fleet and Beowulf laughed joyfully as he plotted his course between the other ships. Already he could see several anxious crews casting a look in their direction as *Wave Dancer* bore down on them in a cloud of spray.

The ship was almost one winter old now and Beowulf was inordinately proud of her. Following his victorious return from Dane Land loaded with the treasure gifted by a grateful King Hrothgar, King Hygelac had confirmed his elevation to ealdorman of the Waegmundings as was his birthright. He had travelled north to the hall of the new king of Swedes, Ohthere, and celebrated the winter solstice and Yule with his betrothed, the king's daughter, Halldis.

Returning to Geatland that spring he had taken his father's old ship, the *Griffon*, down to the town of

33

Domburg in Frisland. It was here that Beowulf had led the men who were to accompany him to confront the monster Grendel as he sought to bond them to one another before they sailed to face the fiend. They had sailed to Britannia to kill a band of *Wealh,* British, pirates and Beowulf had been impressed with the quality and skills shown by the shipbuilders in the port. A purse of gold had been enough to persuade the master builder to stop all other work and construct a dracca in record time for the Geat lord.

Beowulf marvelled at the results of their labours once again from his place on the steering platform as he darted through the ships of the fleet. Fully eighty feet in length and fourteen feet wide athwart the mast, the *Wave Dancer* had rowing stations for fourteen pairs of rowers along each side. Constructed of the finest close grained oak from the great forests of Francland her shallow keel made her ideal for the river work which she was about to undertake on behalf of her people.

Once the ship was complete Beowulf had taken her north to Noregr. There the heavy knarrs, the trading ships, were lightly crewed and a device called a *wind lash* had been developed to compensate for the lack of muscle power in the heavy seas thereabouts. Situated on the steering platform, the wind lash was attached to the ends of the yard by the braces, the ropes which control the angle of the yard to the wind. It was unusual to find a wind lash on a ship in the more heavily manned ships of the southern German Sea but the addition had given the ship its name. By doing the work of half a dozen men, twice as quickly, the sail could be brought into wind in a heartbeat, sending the craft dancing across the waves as others floundered in her wake.

Now, driving before the wind, the *Wave Dancer* bucked
and heaved like a war stallion at full gallop, her great oak
keel groaning and sighing as she threaded her way
through the slowly moving ships to the accompaniment of
cheers, waves and catcalls from the men of the fleet.
Bursting through the last of them like a deer breaking
cover the ship bounded forward and drew swiftly away.

Beowulf looked back at the ships, forging south under
shortened sails and wished them luck. It would be at least
a month before he saw them again.

*

"Well, at least we know our fate if we are not welcome,
lord." Beowulf's hearth warrior, Gunnar, had moved to his
side as the ship wallowed in the ebb tide at the mouth of
the River Wisera. They had arrived in the estuary in the
early evening and, finding the current against them, had
shortened sail and kept station with gentle strokes of the
oars. The *Wave Dancer* was long and lean, as slippery as
any eel, and the waters of the river slid easily past her as
they emptied themselves into the great German Sea
beyond. It was easy work to keep station and the majority
of the crew were lounging amidships as they waited for
the tide to turn and carry them deep into the land of the
Saxons. Beowulf snorted at the comment.

"We have been in far more dangerous situations than
this Gunnar and yet we still live. We have a warloca with
us now," he smiled, "it would be a foolish Saxon who
would risk the displeasure of Woden for the sake of gold
and silver."

Gunnar had been referring to the withy cages and their skeletal inhabitants which stood as a warning to interlopers to the Saxon lands. Fixed on stout wooden stakes, the cages had been set to such a height that they would become submerged by the tide as it ebbed and flowed. Once the cold waters had done their work the attentions of birds, crabs and the elements had quickly reduced the unfortunate occupants to a macabre collection of bleached and weathered bones.

A cry came from amidships and Beowulf smiled as he recognised the braying laugh of his big English hearth warrior, Cola. By the looks of disgust on the faces of the other players his looks had proven deceptive once again and the apparently oafish Englishman was busy scraping his winnings together with his huge paddle-like hands.

More surprising had been the friendship which had struck up between his remaining hearth warrior, the Swede Hrafn, and the Danish warloca Unferth. Unferth had initially been reluctant to accept their presence in the kingdom when they had travelled to Heorot to confront the monster Grendel but, Beowulf had to admit, the holy man had shown great strength of character by publicly admitting his error of judgement.

Beowulf had been frankly shocked when the Dane had arrived at his hall in Geatland that spring. He had confided in him that the Allfather had instructed that he bring the head of the *hel fiend,* Grendel, to the great midsummer ceremonies in the Osning, the holy place, in far off Saxland. Woden had instructed him that he was to ensure that Beowulf escort him in his task and that he remain at the place of worship for the duration of the solstice rites.

To Beowulf's astonishment King Hygelac had waved away his request to leave the planned invasion of Frisland before he had half completed his explanation. Beowulf had expected to lead the ship borne contingent of the army from *Wave Dancer* and he was, he had to admit, more than a little disappointed at his uncle's willingness to lose him from the force, even at the behest of a god. He recognised that his fame had spread throughout the northern lands after the events at Heorot and, later, at the mere of Nykken Force but he reluctantly accepted the fact that the experience in brokering the peace between the Geats and the Swedes after the events at Ravenswood had left him better equipped than most warriors to be tasked with the tactful duty of dealing with the Saxons. He was of course disgruntled nevertheless to be missing the fighting.

The sun was falling away to the West in a blaze of ochre as the tide finally stilled and reversed itself. At the cusp of the change a ship, a fine dracca, had detached itself from the land and swept into mid stream. They watched as the light from the setting sun flashed and danced on the oar blades as, rising and falling in time, the Saxon ship came down upon them. Beowulf had ordered the beast head stowed amidships as they had approached the land to announce to both the land spirits and the watching Saxon warriors that they came with peaceful intent. The Saxons would no doubt be curious as to the identity of the men on this lithe warship, and Beowulf hoped that they would be spending the night ashore once the reason for their journey had been made clear. Beowulf handed the great steering board to Gunnar and donned his red leather war shirt and cloak. Moving to the rear of the steering platform he watched as the Saxon ship master ordered his men to back oars and take the way off the ship as it glided alongside. A broad chested warrior moved to the side of the dracca and Beowulf smiled to himself as he recognised the weather worn, open features which seemed to unite the brotherhood of ship reeves all over the northern kingdoms. The reeve hailed them.

"Welcome to Saxland, lord. My name is Sæfugol. May I ask the reason for your journey to our land?"

Beowulf smiled and announced himself as the Saxon warriors glared at their opposite numbers.

"Sea bird, your reputation is known to me. My name is Beowulf Ecgtheowson. I have been tasked by my king and kinsman, Hygelac of Geatland, with the honour of delivering fine gifts to his brother, King Gewis of the Saxons. I ask that you provide hospitality to myself and my men and provide an escort to your king that we may fulfil our duty to our lord."

Sæfugol smiled happily and inclined his head in respect. Beowulf noticed several of his men shoot an amused glance at one another as he had made his request. He had clearly made a fundamental error in his address but, to his credit, Sæfugol had let it pass. He would have to discover what it was at the earliest opportunity, before he made the same mistake before one less forgiving.

"Beowulf Ecgtheowson, your reputation goes before you, you are welcome in Saxland. All men who seek knowledge have heard the tale of your fight with the fell-monster in Dane land. It would be my honour to provide hospitality for yourself and your crew. Follow us to a berth and I will personally lead you to our hall."

*

Beowulf smiled contentedly as he gazed out across the estuary of the River Wisera. The halls of the Saxons were elevated above the level of the lowlands and commanded far reaching views in all directions. The settlement to which Sæfugol had led the weary Geats consisted of a dozen timber framed halls, each one of which faced inward to a central open area, much like the ones at home save for one point. The majority of these long houses had been constructed to shelter both the people of the settlement and their animals. Apart from the lord's hall which was skirted by a ditch and palisade against raiders, the remainder of the halls had been divided into two. A smaller end housed the owners and their families whilst the longer part of the building was divided into stalls for cattle.

Earlier in the evening Beowulf had entertained the Saxon warriors with the tale of his defeat of the monster Grendel and his *fen-hag* mother. The story was always a great success and the Saxons had listened in awe as he told of the great wrestling match which had taken place between them, both in the hall of the Danish king at Heorot and beneath the fetid mere of Nykken Force. Unferth had produced the head of the fiend at the appropriate time, drawing satisfying gasps from the tough warriors in the hall. Later Beowulf had left the hall and wandered alone around the perimeter of the settlement. It was, he decided, similar in a way to the raised area which contained the Frisian town of Domburg where he had had *Wave Dancer* constructed. Perhaps he mused, all settlements on this coast were built in this way.

Ahead the coastline arced away behind its girdle of low sandy islands to distant Frisland and Beowulf could not but help ponder on the fate of the great ship army he had so recently left. They would have completed their dogleg out to sea by now and would be heading back towards the coast. The Frisian coastguards would gasp in horror as the Geat force would slowly materialise under a great cloud of sail from the early morning sea mist. Riders would hurry inland to alert the defenders but it would be of little use. The *scip here,* the ship army, would be ashore long before any opposing force could assemble, after which the warriors who would remain on board the ships would sail on and enter the great expanse of the Aelmere, bringing fire and sword to the Frisian rear. It was a well thought out plan and he congratulated himself on it. It was, after all, his own.

Below him the low lying coastal lands shimmered as if cloaked under winter ice as the moon, full and bright, painted them with its soft silver sheen. To Beowulf's surprise the lights of men flickered into life like so many stars in the evening sky on the coastline below him and he strolled across to the young warrior keeping a lonely vigil at the head of the path which led down to the strand. The boy glanced across and nodded nervously at the famous Geat lord as he approached and Beowulf smiled as he cast a practised eye over the guard's weapons and mail. The boy was, he estimated, about fifteen winters old and obviously clad in a mail byrnie and helm which had been made for another. The mail hung in a great skirt which approached his knees and the helm made his head appear ludicrously small where it was visible at all. The lack of a sword at his waist and the fact that he was carrying an *angon*, a light throwing spear, instead of the more practical and sturdier stabbing spear, the *framea*, completed the comical image. Obviously, he smiled to himself, the more experienced warriors had clambered to attend tonight's storytelling leaving the boy to guard the shore alone. He recognised the look of apprehension in the young man's features and imagined the thoughts which where whirling around the boy's head at the moment.

That is Beowulf, the killer of Grendel. He is a man of reputation and renown, betrothed to the daughter of the king of Swedes and ealdorman of the Waegmundings. Allfather, please don't let him come across to speak to me!

Beowulf chuckled to himself as he decided to test the boy's resolve. Flicking open the silk 'peace bands' which secured his sword in its scabbard he advanced on the young Saxon. The boy snapped a look down at the hilt of Beowulf's sword and hesitated for a heartbeat.

What will you do young man?

Suddenly the guard made his decision and whirled round to face the threat. As his left foot shot forward to brace his body the angon dropped until it was pointing directly at Beowulf's chest. The wide eyed boy cleared his throat and blurted out the challenge.

Friend or fiend!

Beowulf looked casually down at the point of the angon and glowered at the pale, drawn, face peering up at him from behind his ridiculous helm. "Do you not know who I am Boy?" he snarled, and waited to see how the guard would respond. He was pleased to see the Saxon breathe deeply and compose himself before he replied.

"Yes, lord, but I need you to confirm your identity to me before I let you pass."

Beowulf leaned forward until the point of the angon pricked his chest but the guard still held his weapon firmly and refused to retreat. He was impressed, this boy may look young but his balls had definitely dropped! He made one last try to bully the boy into neglecting his duty.

"What will Sæfugol say when I tell him that one of his men threatened his guest at spear point?"

To Beowulf's delight the boy's resolve remained firm and he kept the angon firmly fixed on him.

"He will say well done, lord. Saxons fear no one."

Beowulf laughed and nodded.

"I can see that. You stood your ground well and I will tell him so. You can relax now, I assure you that I am a friend of the Saxons."

Beowulf indicated the lights on the foreshore. They were clearly causing the guards no concern and he wondered at their purpose.

"They are the local women, lord. They go to the foreshore to collect shellfish when the tides are low."

Beowulf nodded as he understood.

"Just the women?"

"The men are all out fishing, lord," the boy replied. "Since the gods sent the sea to eat at our lands there is very little which is suitable for farming. There are some sheep but very few cattle. Grain and vegetables are traded for dried and salted fish inland, at the markets in Biranum."

Beowulf was surprised. He had seen the large number of stalls in the long houses, perhaps they were intended for horses. The boy shook his head sadly.

"No, they *were* byres for cattle, lord. When the halls were built they overlooked rich farming land but the sea has slowly swallowed it until it is little more than the salt marsh which you see before you. This whole area was populated by one of the most powerful and numerous people during the time when the lands ruled from Rome lay just to the south. We were called the Chaucan and we built these mounds, wierde we call them in our tongue, to keep the settlements safe from storm surges and floods. We were great raiders and warriors but during the time of our great grandfathers we began to move west, across the sea to Britannia. Now only a few of the lowest sort remain in these parts and we are all Saxons."

Beowulf threw the boy a look of surprise.

"Men made all of these hills!"

The Saxon nodded as he looked out across the drowned lands below them.

"Hundreds of years ago, lord. As the sea rose a little higher so the wierde were added to until they reached the level that you see today."

Beowulf looked back across the flooded land as the rasping bark of a vixen carried across the haunting wastes. The sea had ravaged it as brutally as any invading army and for all their ferocity and strength the Chaucan had been powerless against this unrelenting foe.

"You kept saying, 'we'."

The boy turned questioningly to Beowulf.

"Lord?"

"When you were describing the Chaucan you always referred to them as we. Are they your people?"

The guard nodded sadly and stared wistfully across the landscape.

"They were, lord. As I said they are all in Britannia now, my family are one of the few who remain." He indicated the lights on the foreshore. "My mother and sisters will be down there now, lord, with the other women and my father is away fighting in the South. He tries to return every autumn with silver and soon we will join him in Britannia," he said proudly.

Beowulf smiled and turned to go before he hesitated and turned back.

"What is your name?"

"Seaxwine, lord."

"Come and see me before we leave in the morning Seaxwine. I will see if we can at least find you a framea before you really *do* meet a fiend!"

FIVE

They left the place the Saxons knew as Feddersen early the following day. The milky haar, the sea mist which Beowulf had witnessed creeping in on the land the previous evening, had grown thicker during the night and they moved upstream through a landscape washed free of colour.

Sæfugol had bid them farewell from horseback as *Wave Dancer* pulled clear of the jetty and moved into the deeper channel. Glancing back they had watched as the Saxon reeve and his men turned and disappeared back into the mists of their strange land. Beowulf had smiled as one of the smaller riders had proudly raised his new framea in parting before he hurried along in their wake. It had been such a small thing to him but he knew that the gift of the weapon would have raised the standing of the young Saxon amongst his peers and he was glad of it.

As Gunnar went forward and fixed a brand to the stem post to warn other ships of their presence Beowulf reflected on the place they were entering. He had listened incredulously as Sæfugol had explained the organization of the Saxon lands to him over their ale the night before.

The reason for the Saxon warriors amusement when they had arrived had been the use of the title king for the local ruler, Gewis. To Beowulf's astonishment it had been made obvious that the Saxons had no king, the lands being a collection of equal tribes who recognised no overlord. Beowulf had listened attentively as he mentally parcelled up the store of gifts he had been supplied with by the king to lavish on his, assumed, opposite number, as his host chirped happily away.

"We are a loose collection of different tribes, Beowulf. To others we are all Saxons but to ourselves we are still members of the older tribes. I am Chaucan but others here are Chamavian, Reudignian even a few Langbards who remained here in the North whilst the rest of their people migrated south. All the tribes are ruled by their own ealdorling, the equivalent to the rank of ealdorman like yourself. Below them come the farmers and warriors of the freeling, your ceorls, and then the lazzi who you call thralls. Each spring representatives of each tribe gather at a place further upriver called Marklo and travel on to the *heiligen loh*, the holy wood. There, before the great tree of Saxnot, the god of the Saxons, laws are passed and war leaders appointed for the coming year. Saxons jealously guard their freedoms and are wary of those who wish to rule others. As you can see," he had smiled proudly, "we have no need or desire for kings."

Slowly, imperceptibly, the mist began to retreat as the long, low form of the dracca swept upriver and further away from the coast. By mid morning the reed lined banks of the Wisera had appeared, ghostlike, from the gloom as the haar gave way to a light but persistent drizzle. Beowulf finally abandoned the steering duties to

Gunnar and huddled beneath the awning which they had erected amidships in a vain effort to escape the unrelenting damp.

Thankfully the rain had eased off by late morning as a thin, hazy sunshine struggled to impose itself on the world of men. Around the middle of the day a small tree studded island appeared ahead and Beowulf ordered Gunnar to run the ship aground there. Soon the crew had set-to, preparing a hot meal to warm their chilled bodies. As the men sat at their meal they wondered at the steady procession of ships and boats of all shapes and sizes which plied the Wisera. Numerous small craft travelled inland to the markets of the town known as Biranum and they had cast knowing glances to one another as the smell wafting across to the Geats marked them out as fishermen on their way to the markets in the town.

As they prepared to leave and journey on a dozen powerful dracca, the golden dragon of Saxland snapping proudly above them, had pulled past them on their way to the sea. The stern faced warriors had stared to a man at the great golden man and boar flag, Beowulf's personal *herebeacn,* which flew at the masthead of *Wave Dancer* but no challenge had been forthcoming. Obviously, Beowulf mused, they had complete confidence in the ability of Sæfugol and his men to guard the river mouth.

Soon after they had resumed their journey the town of Biranum hove into view. The town was the focus of all shipbuilding activity in Saxland and even from a distance they could see that the waterfront swarmed with activity. On the western side of the town a series of jetties jutted out into the Wisera like so many misshapen teeth whilst further upriver fingers of smoke pointed lazily skyward from the shipyards and smithies which built and repaired the great Saxon fleets. Huddled as it was beneath the scud of smoke which drifted across it, the town was unlike any other the men from the North had seen. It was, as Cola remarked, *'buzzing and heaving like an overturned beehive,'* and Beowulf had to agree with the big Engle. The town seemed to him to encapsulate all the power and vigour of the Saxons within its boundaries.

Coming abreast of the town Beowulf heaved on the big steer board and brought the *Wave Dancer* about. Gunnar rushed to take his place at the stem, ready to guide his lord into an area of the strand which seemed to be kept clear of normal shipping. There was obviously a reason for this, Beowulf knew, but he reasoned that he was on important business and, after all, the *Wave Dancer* could never be classed as normal shipping!

As the ship neared the berth Beowulf was unsurprised to see a group of heavily armed warriors racing along the strand to intercept them. Led by a man who would seem to be the reeve of the town from the quality of his clothing and obvious air of authority, Beowulf and his men watched as the Saxons turned onto the jetty ahead of them and drew to a halt. Beowulf glanced across to Gunnar and indicated that he take the helm.

"Gunnar, take us in will you. Let's see what is getting these Saxons so worked up."

Walking to the side of the ship Beowulf cupped his hand to his mouth and called across the rapidly shrinking gap.

"My name is Beowulf Ecgtheowson, Ealdorman of the Waegmundings. I request a berth in your town and a meeting with Ealdorling Gewis."

To his satisfaction Beowulf noticed that the Saxon warriors exchanged sideways looks with one another as he had announced himself. They clearly knew of him and his reputation. It should help in the upcoming negotiations. He was, however, to be disappointed. If the Saxon reeve was impressed he hid his personal feelings very well. With a wave of his arm he called across to them.

"I am sorry, lord. I must ask you to clear away from the jetty. Biranum is a closed town by order of the ealdorling and these berths are reserved."

Not easily dissuaded, Beowulf called back.

"I have an important matter to discuss with the ealdorling. Can you direct me to a berth where I *can* tie up?"

The reeve shook his head and repeated his request.

"I apologise lord, but I must insist that you leave Biranum. The town is closed to all movement, in or out."

Beowulf turned to Gunnar and nodded pensively. He understood and with a flick of his wrist expertly guided the tall prow of the ship aside. Beowulf cast a look back at the Saxon group and was surprised to see that the reeve had left the protection of his accompanying warriors and was hastening to the end of the jetty. Now that the *Wave Dancer* was headed away from the town this would bring him very close to Beowulf's position at the stern. Gunnar had also noticed the actions of the reeve and used the big oak blade to take the way of the ship. Beowulf walked across to the stern and smiled in welcome as the man approached. To his relief the smile was returned.

At last, I might find out what is going on!

The Saxon approached the end of the jetty and bowed his head slightly in supplication.

"My name is Wilfrid, lord. I am the reeve for the town of Biranum. I can guess at the reason for your desire to meet with the ealdorling but I am afraid that he left the town yesterday in response to the news of the Geat ship army which was reported to be off our coast."

Wilfrid flicked a look along the length of the *Wave Dancer* and Beowulf smiled to himself as he recognised the reeve mentally tallying up the numbers of his crew and their quality. He also noticed that the reeve's gaze had hovered over the awning fastened amidships which covered the gifts which they had brought on their errand.

"Thirty-four tough, battle proven Geat warriors and one Danish warloca," he announced with a grin."Enough to do honour to a Saxon ealdorling but not much of an invasion force Wilfrid!"

The Saxon laughed warmly.

"You must forgive me, lord. We all have our duties to perform."

Wifrid paused, clearly in thought. Beowulf thought that he had gained a measure of the man's qualities during their brief conversation and waited to see what the reeve would say next. Finally he seemed to decide and leaned forward conspiratorially.

"I can see that your duty here is one of peace and can guess the cause of it. Can I ask you which nation your king is intending to attack, lord?"

It was Beowulf's turn to deliberate as he searched his conscience before answering. He was not in the habit of confiding in foreign reeves the detailed intentions of the Geat army but in truth he could see very little harm in this instance. The army had in all probability disembarked in Frisland by now so the secret was no longer. He glanced up at Wilfrid and recognised that the Saxon needed to feel that the exchange of information would be a two way affair before he would divulge any more and anything that he *could* tell the Geat could prove to be very useful.

"A Geat ship army under the command of the king, my kinsman Hygelac, should by now be well established on the shores of northern Frisland. They intend to attack the lands of the Hugas and then move south by land and sea. I have been asked to reassure the ealdorling of Saxland of our peaceful intentions towards their lands by my king. I have also been tasked by Woden, the Allfather, with escorting the warloca Unferth to the midsummer celebration at the Irminsul where he is to sacrifice the head of the monster Grendel to the furious one."

Wilfrid's eyes widened in surprise.

"You have the head of the monster with you?"

Beowulf went to call across to Unferth but the Dane had anticipated the request and was already approaching the steering platform carrying the rune covered box which contained the grisly trophy. Wilfrid beckoned to the Saxon warriors further down the jetty and they hurried up in alarm but the reeve held up a hand to reassure them. As they came up to him he smiled and Beowulf heard his words to them as he beckoned towards the ship.

"We are about to see a thing of which we will tell our grandchildren one day. We are about to see the head of a *hel fiend* displayed by its vanquisher!"

As the Saxons craned their heads forward in anticipation Unferth arrived at the steering platform and flipped up the lid. Reaching inside Beowulf grasped the familiar egg shaped skull and raised it with a flourish. Beowulf chuckled and the guards' jaws dropped as one as Grendel's head came into view. As the Saxons looked on in wonder Beowulf studied the features of his one time adversary. Three winters had passed since that night at Heorot but the head had remained in remarkable condition nevertheless. The lips of the monster had drawn back in death into a hard puckered grin to reveal the line of long dagger-like teeth. Beowulf shuddered slightly as he remembered just how close those teeth had come to removing the right hand side of his face during their struggle. Between them the withered remains of the long serpent-like tongue lolled lazily from between the monster's short wolfish muzzle. The smattering of rough hair which had crowned the grotesque head had long since disappeared, he noted, but the waxy reptilian skin and long elfish ears of the troll if anything looked even more monstrous than they had in life.

Replacing the head in the box, Beowulf thanked Unferth and turned back to the Saxons who were now regarding him with a sense of awe.

"I am sure that you will agree that Grendel's head is an impressive sight, one which I am sure that the ealdorling would be disappointed to have missed." He paused to let the remark sink in before continuing. "Perhaps you could direct me to the place where I can find him?"

*

Dayraven kicked the crewman in the guts and repeated the question.

"How many men are there in Dorestada?"

The Geat doubled up in pain and coughed a bloody gobbet of phlegm onto the sun bleached deck.

"Why don't you go and count them," he gasped before flicking a look up at the Frisian's war helm. "Or you could ask your chicken to fly over and have a look for you."

Dayraven removed his helm and stroked the raven wings which adorned its crest.

"Now *you* are a very funny man," he smiled, menacingly. "Let's see if you can still find something to laugh about with Ran. I am sure that the sea goddess enjoys a good joke as well as any mortal."

Dayraven indicated that his men toss the Geat over the side with a flick of his head. Two Frisian warriors stepped forward and, grinning, bundled the bound man overboard. The Geat floated just long enough to hurl a final insult at the Frisian leader before he sank to the bottom of the Aelmere, joining the rest of his crew.

"Bastard chicken head!"

Dayraven shrugged nonchalantly as the Fris warriors looked to gauge his reaction.

"Funny *and* brave. Ran *will* be pleased."

SIX

Beowulf sat back and took another pull on the skin of ale which the Saxons had provided. Riversides had always been one of his favourite locations to spend a lazy day and this was even better than most. Below the terrace on which the Geat party had established themselves lay the great rope yards of the town of Honovere, a hive of activity like every place they had passed through on their journey inland. Yes, he reflected, there were few better ways to spend a day than drinking and eating in the sun as others worked and sweated below you.

Wave Dancer had arrived at the town the previous day and they had reported their presence to the reeve as was customary. Naturally the man had been expecting them and a guest hall had already been assigned for their use. There the hall steward, Godwin, had informed him that ealdorling Aldwulf had requested that they await his return from the holy wood which would be in two days time. Godwin had informed Beowulf that a special meeting of all the ealdorling had been convened to discuss the Saxon response to any incursion by the ship army off their coast into their lands and Beowulf had immediately realised the wisdom which King Hygelac had shown by dispatching his renowned nephew to placate them. He had seen for himself the strength and vigour of the Saxons and marvelled at the speed with which they had reacted to the potential threat which had suddenly appeared. He was under no illusion as to the disaster which would result should the great Saxon army fall upon the flank of the Geatish forces.

Once the reeve at Biranum had recovered from the excitement which Grendel's head had caused them he had been more forthcoming with details of the Saxon response to this mystery ship army. Apparently the Geatish fleet had been spotted by one of the Saxon vessels which routinely patrolled the coast and the dracca had hurried in to the fortress of Hamma Burg which lay on the River Albia in the northern part of Saxland. The ealdorling there had immediately dispatched riders to inform his peers, with a request that they meet at the holy wood to elect a war leader and discuss their response to the threat. Wilfrid had explained that all men of the freeling class of warrior-farmer who owned ten hides of land or more were required to keep a horse for use as a remount by the ealdorling messengers so the news had travelled swiftly through the land. Within three days of sighting the fleet the Saxon leaders had convened and were making their plans beneath the great statue of Saxnot.

Beowulf had hurried on with the intention of travelling to the meeting place and explaining that the designs of his king carried no threat to them. The holy wood lay to the west of a place the Saxons called Marklo. Conveniently the town was situated on the River Wisera, the very river they were travelling along, and with such a fine ship and crew Beowulf had no doubt that the thirty miles could be covered by mid morning the following day. Their spirits had lifted further as the sun forced its way through to burn off the mist which seemed to hang about the coastal marshes like a heavy cloak. As the banks of the Wisera slowly drew together and the land grew firmer, the soils deeper, the landscape slowly transformed itself. The pale yellows and browns of the heath lands and reed beds receded in their wake to be replaced by the first trees. Alder and willow appeared and the staccato beat of the woodpecker began to replace the booming of the bittern. Deer began to be glimpsed hidden amongst the shadowy thickets, and a small herd of bison had paused from drinking at the bank to watch them sweep by.

They had, however, been disappointed in their goal. As the *Wave Dancer* had neared Marklo the river divided and a group of heavily manned dracca had appeared in their path, barring the way. It had no longer surprised the Geat that they were waiting for his arrival and despite his best efforts the Saxon warrior leading the group had steadfastly refused to let them pass. The man had been friendly but firm as he had insisted that they were to take the River Alera which snaked away to their left before joining the River Leina, the rope river, which would lead them up to Honovere where they were to await the return of the ealdorling. All of Beowulf's attempts to remain on the Wisera had been politely rebuffed and he had been impressed once again by the mettle displayed by individual Saxons when he had tried to intimidate them. He had first encountered it in the young boy Seaxwine and he had found that he was coming to admire their seemingly unshakable sense of self worth.

Beowulf was dragged back from his reverie as a peel of laughter rolled around the waterfront. He followed the gaze of his men across to the *Wave Dancer* and was unsurprised to see that his man Cola seemed to be the centre of all attention. He turned to Cola's fellow hearth warrior, Hrafn, who was chuckling at his side.

"Cola is doing his old trick and hurling children into the air, lord," he explained with a grin.

Gunnar, Cola and a few others had stayed with the ship due to the amount of interest it had generated in the town. Beowulf had left his personal flag of the man fighting the boar at the masthead and the unfamiliar design was attracting widespread interest. In no time a crowd had gathered to admire the sleek lines of the strange foreign ship and Gunnar and a few others had volunteered to show people around. Their efforts were proving to be a great success with the workers and their families and Beowulf joined in the laughter as another child sailed high into the air. This time Cola turned away as the child began to plummet back towards the deck as he responded to a question from Gunnar. Beowulf and Hrafn chuckled as a horrified gasp came from the watching men and women. They had seen the trick many times before and knew that the child was in no danger. At the last moment Cola spun around and plucked the apparently doomed child from the air. The crowd roared with laughter as they realised that it had all been part of the show, and they all watched as Cola handed the boy back to his delighted mother with a friendly tousle of his hair. Hrafn glanced across with a smile.

"We should have sent Cola on his own to keep the Saxons happy, lord," he joked. "We didn't need the treasure after all, shall we keep it?"

Beowulf glanced up as a shadow fell across him to find that Aldwulf's hall steward had joined them and was laughing as hard as any at the antics on the waterfront.

"Godwin!" he smiled, "will you join us?"

Godwin looked down and pulled a wry smile.

"I would like that a great deal, lord," he sighed. "Unfortunately I will be rather busy. A rider has just arrived from holy wood to inform me that that the ealdorling will be returning this evening after all and I am to arrange a *symbel* in your honour. I just came down to warn you to prepare for a riotous evening."

*

The pink glow of dusk was beginning to throw its light through the open doors of the guest hall as Godwin reappeared to summon them into the presence of his lord. Aldwulf had arrived back from the holy wood earlier that evening as promised and had gone straight into the main hall with the men of his comitatus. The Geats had returned to their hall as soon as they had been made aware of the expected arrival of the ealdorling where they had donned their war gear and awaited the call. It had been a long afternoon of waiting and it was with more than a little relief that they had finally responded to the summons to the main hall.

Beowulf had finally decided that he would don his red battle shirt above his mail byrnie. To be truthful it was an added encumbrance that he could do without at a formal drinking celebration like a symbel but, on balance, he decided that the shirt was too impressive to leave off. Made of thick leather, the battle coat had been boiled in a wax to which the blood of an ox had been added before it had been carefully shaped to fit his body. It was the perfect background on which to display his gold belt buckle and fittings while the cloisonne work of the heavy gold shoulder clasps which held the shirt together never failed to impress.

Gunnar had spent a good part of the afternoon rolling his mail shirt in a barrel of sand and it now gleamed like newly polished silver, while the whole was set off by a fine, boar capped, helm. He had chosen to wear the open fronted helm which had been a gift from King Hygelac after he had defeated the Grendel. It was as fine a helm as existed on middle earth and was much more suitable for such occasions than the closed face grim helm which he wore in battle.

He glanced back as the men took station on him and smiled at the appearance of the warloca, Unferth. The Dane had travelled with them dressed in the plainer clothes of an everyday warrior but he had risen to the occasion Beowulf noted gratefully and had chosen to don the appearance of the holy man which he was for the symbel. The other warriors had looked on with mounting unease as the man had transformed himself slowly into the personification of a raven. The transformation now complete, Beowulf looked on the warloca with a mixture of approval and disquiet. Dressed completely in black Unferth wore a cloak of raven feathers which shimmered and gleamed as they moved in the last of the dying days light. The Dane had used a mixture of ash from the hearth to grind a paste which he had applied to his face to darken it whilst a red mixture had been applied around his eyes. Beowulf had subtly exchanged looks of incomprehension with the men as Unferth had muttered incantations as he continued to apply the mixture. The holy man's actions seemed to be only a part of the transformation and their questions had been answered as soon as Godwin had arrived to summon them into Aldwulf's presence. Unferth had gone across to a wolf skin bag and removed an item which resembled the top half of a giant raven skull. Completely covering the top half of the man's head, the beak of the raven extended almost one foot in front of his face whilst the top and sides of the headpiece were covered in the same raven feathers as the cloak.

Turning to Beowulf with a smile which seemed suddenly bereft of warmth, Unferth had, it would seem, now totally transformed himself from the easygoing companion they had grown accustomed to on this journey to a man who demanded fear and respect in equal measure. Unferth took up his raven skull tipped staff and indicated that the warriors carry the box containing Grendel's head into the hall in his wake. Beowulf glanced back at Godwin to indicate that they were ready and was amused to see that the warloca's transformation had had the desired affect on the hall steward. It could only help their cause to have the gods clearly on their side.

Beowulf's hearth warriors, Gunnar and Cola, moved forward to flank their lord as they emerged into the wide courtyard which stood before the main hall. They could not help but notice that the number of horses which were corralled to the far side of the hall had increased dramatically since their confinement and the low hum which seemed to emanate from the hall before them confirmed to Beowulf that the building was likely to be packed with Saxon warriors.

Beowulf regarded the gable end of the hall of Ealdorman Aldwulf as he approached. It was very similar he thought, in many ways, to the great hall of the Swedes in far off Uppsala. Built from massive oak posts from the surrounding wild wood the frames between the posts had been in-filled with a mixture of wattle and daub. Carved figures which clearly represented Woden, Thunor and Saxnot, guarded the entrance to the hall but other than those there seemed to be very little decoration. The whole had been lime washed repeatedly until the building seemed to shine with a brilliant whiteness which caused it to stand out in stark contrast with its surroundings. He had noticed a similar hall in Biranum which he now knew must have been the hall of Ealdorling Gewis. It was, he thought, an effective and powerful statement to visitors of the strength and solidarity of this kingless land.

Lazzi stepped forward to take the Geats' weapons as they approached the doors of the hall. Beowulf was always reluctant to disarm himself but he recognised the practicalities involved in avoiding bloodshed in such situations. Copious amounts of ale and egotistical warriors would be a heady mix at any time. With the potential for heightened tensions between the parties due to the presence of a marauding Geat army nearby a word said out of place could have fatal consequences for both their mission and, quite possibly, themselves. With a final roll of his shoulders Beowulf stepped forward and crossed the threshold of the hall.

Godwin led the Geat party forward towards the gift stool, the high seat, of Ealdorling Aldwulf which lay at the far end of the hall. As Beowulf's eyes became accustomed to the smoky interior the familiar details of a great hall revealed themselves to him. Flanking a central hearth which ran the length of the hall lay benches packed with Saxon warriors. The walls were lined with colourful hangings which told of the deeds of the gods and, it would appear, great Saxon victories in battle. Motes of dust danced among the blades of light which cut down from openings high in the walls. A golden beam passed over his head from behind, painting the great battle flag of the Saxons which hung suspended in the place of honour to the rear of the ealdorling's gift stool with its buttery hue.

Ahead of him stood Aldwulf flanked by his thegns, Saxon lords dressed for war, the last rays of the dying sun gleaming and flashing from their burnished war gear. Beowulf allowed himself a slight snort of amusement as he recognised that the moment which they had been invited to the hall had been carefully chosen by the Saxons. It had been no accident, he knew, that the moment had been chosen which would present the lord and his men in, quite literally, the most dazzling light. They did, he had to admit to himself, look highly impressive.

Aldwulf was a man of about forty winters, tall and broad with features which time and countless campaigns had worked to fashion into a formidable cast. If the man's countenance seemed belligerent his eyes told a different story. Beowulf had long ago learned that the eyes were the wind hole to the soul and Aldwulf's shone with warmth and good humour. To Beowulf's unexpected pleasure the

Saxon moved forward and, smiling openly, extended the hand of friendship to him.

"Welcome to Saxland, Beowulf Ecgtheowson," he began, "I have heard many good things about your exploits, both in the North and in Britannia." Aldwulf gripped Beowulf by the shoulders and grinned. "I greet you as an equal, Ealdorman of the Weagmundings. Come and take ale with me and avail yourself of Saxon hospitality. We are looking forward to the tale of how you killed the monster in Dane Land!"

Aldwulf glanced across to the gifts which Beowulf's men were carrying.

"You didn't need to bring us gifts if you were going to attack the Fris and the Francs," he laughed, "we would have shipped treasure to you if you would have agreed to do it!"

*

The Saxon hall steward had assured them of a riotous evening ahead and his lord had more than lived up to the promise. Beowulf had felt relaxed and welcome from the moment that he had arrived in the town of Honovere and the hospitality provided by the ealdorling had been lavish and varied.

Beowulf was pleased to see that his men had been allowed to mix freely with the Saxon warriors and both parties were clearly enjoying the opportunity to trade tales of the many battles and lands which they had experienced.

Beowulf had asked Aldwulf for permission to introduce the 'story barrel' which he had first experienced during his time as a *wrœcca*, an exile, in Swede Land. A barrel was produced and upended in the centre of the hall. The men then took turns to stand on the barrel and share an experience which they had with the warriors in the hall.

Beowulf had elected to go first and told the tale of the fight with the trolls in northern Swede Land. The tale was always well received and it gave him the opportunity to pass around his magnificent gold handled gladius which he had used to kill the giant.

Hrafn had told the tale of the great battle at Ravenswood. Rightly famous throughout the northern lands it had witnessed the deaths of two kings and Beowulf's own father. He had honoured Beowulf, his lord, by recounting the manner of his father's death, fighting whilst blinded at the forefront of the Swedish boar snout. By a quirk of wyrd Hrafn had been the only one of the Swedish King Ongentheow's hearth warriors to survive and he had held the rapt attention of the Saxons as he recounted his tale of that fateful day.

As each man completed his tale and stepped down he called on the next man to take his place. Many of the Saxon warriors told tales of their campaigns in Britannia and amongst the Francs. Beowulf was astonished to discover that despite the apparent Saxon aversion to rule by kings, a Saxon called Aelle seemed to have established a kingdom in all but name to the south of the Jutish kingdom of Cent in Britannia. A few of the warriors present had lived and fought there against the Wealas before returning home heavy with riches and reputation.

As the evening wore on Beowulf and his men had been ushered outside to witness a display by a party of Huns. They had watched in awe as the arrows loosed by the small men with their strange shaped bows had easily punched through the shields and mail which had been set up on the far side of the courtyard. It was the first time that he had seen members of that people and he was amazed at the similarity between their high cheek boned features and those of Kaija, the Sami volva back home in the temple at Miklaborg.

The highlight of the evening was of course Beowulf's description of the fight with the monsters at Heorot, Grendel and his mother. Unferth had played his part as he had produced the grotesque head of the fiend at the appropriate time to the accompaniment of gratifying gasps of amazement from the watching Saxons.

Aldwulf finally revealed that he had been authorised by the war council to inform Beowulf that as long as the Geat army respected the Saxon border which ran along the Rivers Emesa, Isla, Rin and Lupia, that no Saxon army would interfere with their raid. He would provide an escort for Beowulf and his party as far as the settlement known as Theotmalli. From there it was but a short ride into the Osning, the holy place, where the Irminsul was located. Following the ceremonies it would be an easy matter to follow the course of the River Lupia to the mighty Rin, on the northern reaches of which stood the Frisian settlement of Dorestada, Beowulf's ultimate goal.

Tired but elated the Geats had finally retired to their hall as the new day flashed crimson in the eastern sky. It was less than one week now to the midsummer celebrations at the Irminsul and they really did need to complete their journey. Beowulf knew better than most that Woden, the furious one, was not a god to accept disappointment lightly.

SEVEN

Hygelac was momentarily stunned by the news from his ealdorman but, realising that all eyes would be on him for his reaction, he quickly snapped back to the matter at hand which was, he now knew, survival. His mind raced as he tried to think of a reply for the man, with the Francish front line now only moments away. Suddenly, almost magically, his mind cleared and his decision was made. He recognised the sword peace which came over him at such moments and knew that it was a gift from Woden. He managed a smile to himself despite his apparently precarious situation. The Allfather had not deserted him yet. He grinned encouragingly at the obviously shaken messenger and tapped the man's framea with his own.

"What is your name?"

The young warrior looked confused at his king's reply but managed to stammer.

"Bjorn, lord."

Hygelac could already hear the tramp of Francish feet as the army of King Theodoric came upon them. He deliberately moved onto the bridge and turned his back scornfully on the approaching fiend as he continued his conversation. He knew that the ranks of Geats to each side of the bridge, protected as they were by the deeply channelled rivulet, would be looking at the point of contact and watching the actions of their king and he flashed a glance to his left to see their reaction. They were, to a man, smiling at his confident action and he calmly replied to the messenger.

"Well, Bjorn, it would seem that we could use a bear today. Come and fight with me and you can tell your grandchildren the tale when you are old and grey!"

Bjorn joined the smiling men of his king's comitatus and advanced onto the bridge. Hygelac called a halt at the midpoint where the roadway rose slightly to allow boats free passage beneath. It was a perfect position, only twenty paces wide and flanked by solid walls of stone. The earlier rain shower had left a greasy film on the cobbled surface of the roadway which would make the uphill fight of the Francs all the harder.

Hygelac beat his framea on his shield rim and cried a challenge which was echoed by his hearth warriors. Within a heartbeat it had been taken up by the Geat shield wall, a crescendo of noise which seemed to roll along its length in waves.

Satisfied now in the strength of his men and their deployment Hygelac took up the position of honour at the mid point in the front rank of the wall of shields, the white boar of Geatland snapping proudly above him in the freshening breeze.

At his command the men on the bridge heft their shields and framea and took up the position with a cry.

Left foot forward and braced, shields' interlocking, spears raised and ready.

And then, just as the leading Francs neared the far side of the bridge, the dogs came.

*

Hygelac watched, bemused, as the enemy line slowed briefly and bunched together. Suddenly, from their midst burst forth a dozen of the largest, most ferocious dogs that he had ever seen. Their massive, slathering heads and broad powerful forequarters were encased in a shell of leather armour. Around their neck was fixed a collar studded with long, wickedly sharp, metal spikes.

Hygelac and the men of his comitatus looked on in horror as the war dogs bounded clear of the Francish line and came on at them in a silence heavy with menace.

Hygelac was the first to recover from the shock and his mind and body reacted to the unfamiliar threat in a heartbeat. Sinking to his knees he cried out to the shocked Geats.

"Front rank fall to one knee. Skewer them in the belly as they leap at the shield wall!"

Hygelac prepared his thrust as the men to either side of him crashed down beside him. The dogs were close enough now that he could tell which animal would be his target and he threw his left shoulder behind his shield as he waited for the time to strike. Hygelac gripped his spear tightly as the beast loped silently on, the folds of loose skin on its face rising and falling as it came.

With a snarl the dog leapt and Hygelac slammed his right arm forward with all his strength. The framea slid into the unprotected belly of the dog and plunged through, liquidising its innards as it did so. The animal let out a high pitched yelp and fell in front of the wall. Hygelac screamed out above the mayhem as the Francs gained the entrance to the bridge.

"Front rank up and draw swords!"

The Geats rose up as one and braced themselves to receive the charge which was now only moments away. Hygelac savagely kicked the mortally wounded dog before him out into the path of the onrushing Francish warriors. Far from crashing into the Geat shield wall and leaving it in disarray the attack by the war dogs had merely succeeded in littering the narrow roadway with dead and dying bodies, the hedge of spears protruding from the howling animals only adding to the defence.

Realising the effect that the unexpected obstacle would have on the Francish charge Hygelac yelled his last command before the shields clashed.

"Hold this line. Let them come to us!"

Seeing the obstacles before them the leading Francs, led by a man in magnificent scale armour which seemed to ripple and flow as he moved, leapt across the writhing bodies and crashed into the Geat front line. Hygelac brought his shield across and swept the framea of his opponent up and away as he landed. Already off balance the Francs' defence was opened up by the move and Hygelac quickly took advantage, stabbing his sword down into the area of the man's unprotected middle. The blade slid through leather and flesh as it passed deeply inside. Shaking the screaming man from his sword Hygelac braced himself for the next attack. A groin wound was instantly debilitating and agonisingly painful and Hygelac knew that the strike would add another thrashing, pain filled body to the growing barrier before them.

The king sensed the blades of his men's swords flicking out to the left and right as he watched the enemy attack begin to descend into confusion and chaos. He started as a bloodied face appeared before him and instinctively pulled his head to one side as the shaft of a framea flicked forward to transfix the man's throat.

Ahead, the Francs were beginning to hesitate as they reached the bloody barrier which separated them from their enemy and appeared to be almost panic stricken as they attempted to wend their way through the obstacles which stood between the two sides. Suddenly two huge warriors seemed to appear from nowhere and burst through the growing pile of bodies which littered the roadway. Hygelac braced for the considerable impact as the Francish giants crashed into him but, to his surprise, no contact came. His head darted from behind his shield just in time to see the enemy ranks open up to swallow the pair as they carried the badly wounded man in scale armour to the rear.

The action seemed to signal the end of the attack and the Francs began to back away from them. Sensing an opportunity to score a morale boosting victory in front of the watching armies Hygelac instinctively knew that the time had come to carry the fight to them. One big push should chase them off he reasoned and with a cry of "Geats!... Geats!" he vaulted the miserable collection of dead and dying.

He had judged the moment to perfection and the Francs broke and ran as the men of Hygelac's comitatus, his hearth warriors, poured across to support their lord. They halted at the end of the bridge and watched the retreating Francs tumble back across the field. Behind them the massed ranks of the Geat shield wall roared and called their acclamation of the small knot of men who had won the victory against the odds.

As the enemy left the field Hygelac's hearth warrior, Ealhstan, turned and looked across with a look of puzzlement.

"If they darken the meadow with their numbers, lord, why did they attack with so few?"

As Hygelac made to reply Wulf, Ealhstan's colleague, supplied the answer. Along with Thurgar and Tofi the pair carried the rings on the hilts of their swords which marked them out as warriors of the special brotherhood which had accompanied Beowulf to Dane Land to kill the Grendel. They were close friends but delighted their colleagues with their constant ribbing of one another.

"Because, my witless friend, I suspect that you just witnessed what happens when a young member of the royal family takes it into their head to gain himself a reputation by chasing off the wicked *fiend* before his elders arrive and steal all the glory. Little did he know that we had just enlisted the aid of Bjorn the bear and all he got for his trouble was a spear in the arse!"

They all laughed and turned to the slightly built messenger and found him examining the gory tip of his framea and grinning like a fool. He did not, Hygelac suddenly realised, have the look of a typical warrior and a thought suddenly struck him.

"Have you ever fought in the front rank before Bjorn?"

"No, lord," Bjorn answered, clearly both surprised and elated to have survived the onslaught, "I have never fought anywhere. Ealdorman Hromund said that he needed all the warriors to defend the bridge."

Wulf and Ealhstan grinned as Hygelac began to comprehend that he had entrusted his life to an inexperienced boy.

"But I recognised the colours on your spear shaft as it shot past my ear and took that Franc in the throat."

"Yes, lord!" Bjorn beamed proudly.

"So what work do you normally do, if you are not a warrior?"

Wulf and Ealhstan could retain their composure no longer and collapsed into laughter at the bemused expression on the king's face. They clearly already knew Bjorn's identity and were revelling in their lord's confusion.

"I work in the kitchens with Flosi," he replied. "I prepare the vegetables, lord."

*

After the initial furore of activity the army of the Francs proceeded to leisurely make camp half a mile from the Geat position. The acres of pasture became a whirl of activity as the thralls and common warriors worked feverishly to construct, what looked to the watching Geats, to be a long term camp. Tofi had trotted across from his position further down the line during the lull and motioned across to the enemy camp which was rapidly taking shape.

"Do you think that they are going to lay siege to us, lord?"

Hygelac shrugged.

"It's a possibility. It's not as if we are going anywhere in a hurry, after all." He conceded gloomily. "They must know that we have very little, if any, food with us and no fresh water. Even if we drink from the river they can easily fill the upper courses with dead cattle and sheep and let them float down on us."

He turned to his hearth warrior and prised his helm from his head.

"Here wear this for a while. I need to speak with Hromund and I want our friends across there to think that I am still here."

Hygelac made his way back through the lines offering words of encouragement to the men as he did so. To a man they smiled happily as he passed them and he was thankful that they appeared to be either fatalistic or mad. Unless Woden intervened on their behalf, as far as he could see they were already dead men.

Retrieving his mount from the place where they had been corralled Hygelac trotted down to Hromund's position at the lower bridge. As he did so he cast a practised eye over the situation there. The Geats clearly still held the bridge in force and enough warriors had been distributed along the riverbank to deter any opportunistic crossing attempts. To the rear Hromund had collected a large reserve of warriors which could quickly react to any threat from the large Frisian army which had gathered in Dorestada.

As he came up to them he found that Hromund had been alerted to his imminent arrival and stood waiting to report the situation to his king. Hygelac dismounted and smiled ironically at his ealdorman's happy greeting.

"We seem to have upset the locals, lord!"

Hygelac snorted and took the horn of ale he had been offered. Downing the contents in one long draught he wiped his beard and grinned at his friend.

"That was the best ale that I have ever tasted. Have you been keeping a secret supply from us?"

Hromund laughed and glanced across to a collection of wagons which had been drawn together and placed under guard to one side of the meadow.

"I managed to scoop up the supplies and get them across the bridge before the Fris arrived. We have enough food and ale for about a week, lord."

Hygelac clapped him delightedly on the arm as he saw the first glimmer of light appear amongst the storm clouds which had suddenly broken upon them. Hromund indicated with a slight shift of his head that the king follow him to a quieter spot. Each man grabbed up a hunk of pork from the table there and slowly strolled across the water meadow. Hygelac was the first to speak.

"I have already repulsed one attack on the southern bridge with ease. If we can hold them off until night falls we can mount up and attempt a breakout."

Hromund smiled sadly and shook his head. He stopped and turned to face him.

"Not this time old friend, this is where our story ends. Every man here knows it but they will all fight to the end nevertheless."

Hygelac made to protest but his friend put up a hand to stop him.

"Do you remember that time when we dared each other to go into the bear cave and kick the sleeping bear in the arse?" he smiled.

Hygelac laughed at the memory. They had been boys then, six or seven winters old and they had stumbled upon the cave of a hibernating bear on the hill known as the Troll's Hat. The ealdorman of nearby Edet had a fine hunting lodge there and the boys had been given free rein to explore the forests between hunts. He turned to Hromund with some of the old vigour of youth restored.

"Listen. Now that we have supplies we can either break out in one single overwhelming body or we can slip men through under the cover of darkness and tell Heardred to return with the rest of the army. He could be back here inside a week. Then we can chase these bastards off like we have all summer, you have seen their mettle."

To his disappointment Hromund remained grim faced.

"What will happen if we get through? Geats don't run back to their ships with their tails between their legs, lord. And what would happen if your son Heardred returned with the rest of the army? Even if we prevailed against such overwhelming odds, our nation would have lost the best part of it's fighting men and the Swedes will be living in our halls and harvesting our crops within the month." He smiled and shook his head at his friend the king. "Our wyrd is to die here. You leave your kingdom well provided with an heir and enriched beyond measure. Ealdorman Beowulf will marry the king of Swede Land's daughter and ensure our borders are respected."

Hromund tossed the gristly end of the pork to an expectant dog and wiped the grease from his hands on his tunic. Turning to face the king he smiled warmly and clasped him on the arm as he completed his appraisal.

"Woden in his wisdom has given us the opportunity to make an end to our story which will ring down the ages, lord. For as long as men gather in smoky halls to entertain each other with tales of great men the name of Hygelac can stand alongside Sigurd and Arminius, Attila and Alexander. Our days will not end dribbling soup and spending more time pissing than sleeping every night as old age slowly eats at us."

Hromund pointed to a barrel of ale and indicated that one of the guards bring it across. As the man hastened over he completed his advice to his king.

"Stop thinking like a king and revert to the warrior you always were Hygelac. You cannot change the end which the gods have in store for us and every man here knows it. You are no longer responsible for us, each man must die in the manner in which he deems fit and that includes you." Hromund put his arm around the shoulders of his old friend. "Help me finish this barrel and take the rest up to the men, they deserve it. The next time we sup, we sup in valhall!"

*

Hygelac reflected on his friend's words as he rode slowly back to the main shield wall. To his surprise once he had accepted the wisdom of Hromund's words his mood lightened considerably. In fact, he realised, he felt practically elated once the burden of responsibility had been lifted from him. The men in the ranks turned as word passed amongst them that their king had apparently rustled up a supply of food and ale for them and they turned and cheered him as he regained the top of the rise. Behind him the wagons rumbled away to each side and men passed the meat and drink through their ranks accompanied by a buzz of good natured anticipation.

Hygelac acknowledged the happy, smiling faces of his hearth warriors as he regained his position and flicked a look along the line of warriors to each side. To a man they were laughing and joking as they tucked in to their unexpected last meal and he felt proud and humbled to end his days with such men.

To his side Wulf belched as he lowered his horn of drink and indicated ahead.

"Movement to the front, lord. It looks as though they might be coming out to play again."

Hygelac turned his gaze to the front and saw a group of riders emerge from the Francish positions. Small men with long dark moustaches were approaching the Geats on some of the smallest, most ridiculous looking horses that they had ever seen. Despite the warmth of the day each man seemed to be wearing a small round hat made of fur and they watched, incredulous, as the horses skipped along with short, lightning-fast, steps. Hygelac smiled delightedly and called across to Tofi.

"Tofi, toss me my helm. It looks as though the fun is starting again."

EIGHT

Beowulf crested the rise and reined in his mount as a cry penetrated the scanty tree cover. Raising his gaze he squinted into the deep cerulean sky searching for the eagle he knew would be there and was rewarded by the sight of the magnificent bird soaring high on outstretched wings.

Ahead of him the track plunged downwards, back into the gloomy embrace of the wald and he sighed as he waited for the others to come up. Riding across the Saxon lands were akin to sailing a ship across the northern seas, he mused, one long green roller after another!

They had left Honovere several days previously after bidding farewell to Gunnar and the rest of the crew as they had pulled away from the waterfront. *Wave Dancer* was heading back to the German sea where she would turn her prow northwards for home. Beowulf, Cola and Hrafn were travelling on alone to link up with the army at Dorestada once they had discharged their duty to Woden and escorted Unferth to the midsummer celebration at the Irminsul. To his disappointment Beowulf knew that his chance for any serious fighting was receding by the day but, in truth, he had enjoyed his visit to Saxland and he knew that there would be plenty of opportunities to quarrel with his king's enemies in the future. He was sure that Hygelac's raid would be the first of many.

Gunnar had sailed the lakes and rivers of Swede land as a youth and he had never lost his love of life on the water. His abilities as ship master had first become apparent on the way to Uppsala to raid the Swedes. Later they had traversed the great northern seas in midwinter as they sought to bring chaos to King Hythcyn's Yuletide celebrations and Gunnar had become a vital addition to the crew of the *Puffin*, the knarr which they had chartered in Trondelag to carry them south. The wind and waves had been terrifying on the trip and Beowulf reasoned that any man who could handle a ship in mountainous seas and roaring gales with such aplomb, garnering the respect of the tough no-nonsense crew as he did so, would be the ideal choice for ship master when the time came and he owned his first dracca. To Beowulf's delight Gunnar had leapt at the chance and, although he would miss the man's intelligence and ability he knew that there were few men better qualified for the charge.

It had been a strange feeling to stand on foreign soil and watch his much loved ship and crew receding a little more with each gentle stroke of the oars. The ridiculous idea had stolen into his mind that he would never see the ship or its crew again and a strange melancholy had overtaken him as the ship had doubled the bend to the North. The great sweep of *Wave Dancer*'s stern post had been slowly swallowed by the alder trees which crowded the bank there and it had been with difficulty that he had shaken the mood as they had crossed the River Leina and joined the track which led west.

Beowulf twisted in the saddle and smiled as his Saxon companion came up.

"Fresh bread and sausage," the man grinned, "not things which a Saxon can easily ride past, lord!"

Waldhere was one of Ealdorling Aldwulf's thegns. Beowulf had resurfaced from the guest hall at Honovere as the sun approached its high point to find a party of warriors waiting patiently for them under the shade of a large tree. He had recognised their leader as one of Aldwulf's leading thegns from the symbel the previous evening and the man had smiled warmly and indicated a bevy of saddled and readied horses which had clearly been provided for their use. In no time he had rousted his companions and their journey to the Osning had commenced.

Beowulf had quickly come to enjoy Waldhere's companionship. The man had an open, easy-going, manner and Beowulf recognised the judgement which the ealdorling had shown when he had appointed the man to guide them to Theotmalli. Waldhere indicated the road ahead as he offered Beowulf a hunk of bread and sausage.

"One more ridge today and we will reach the last hall of our journey. We will reach Theotmalli the following day and then it will just a matter of following the crowds to the midsummer celebrations." Waldere paused and shot Beowulf a wicked grin. "Just one more rendition of the man against the monster tale and you will be free, lord."

Beowulf returned the smile and chuckled. It was true that he was growing weary of recounting the same tale night after night but the gasps of wonder which the head of the monster invariably drew from the watching warriors had never lost their appeal to him. The events at

Heorot and Nykken Force had caused his reputation to soar to almost mythical heights in the halls of the northern lands and, he reasoned, the more men who actually saw the physical head of Grendel the more his tale would be believed. Woden had helped him to establish the reputation which he had craved since childhood and it would seem that the god now required a small measure of repayment. If he could use this trip to enhance his standing amongst the Saxons all the better but, he mused, he had actually become quite attached to the macabre trophy and he would be sorry to see the head of the fiend depart forever.

"It's strange," he replied, "but sometimes those events seem to be a dream, even to me. When Unferth turned up carrying Grendel's head it was almost like meeting an old friend again!"

Waldere tore a length from the sausage with his teeth and shot Beowulf a cheeky grin.

"Remind me not to upset any of your old friends then, lord!" he winked.

They laughed together as the horses picked their way down through the sun dappled pathway which stretched out ahead of them. Soon, inevitably, the ancient oaks and elm closed in on the group once more as they dipped down and plunged back into the dense tree cover.

The cool of the shade came as a welcome relief to the pale skinned northerners as Beowulf breathed in the sights and smells of the Saxon wald. The weather had rapidly grown warmer the further they had travelled from the coastal lands and the heat of the sun on their skin was becoming painful. Cola had slept on one side at a rest stop and promptly burned one side of his face so badly that he now resembled an enormous red and white dog, much to the other warriors amusement. Luckily the man had an enormous capacity for self depreciation and Beowulf could hear him happily discussing the relative merits of Frisian and Saxon pies further back along the column with one of Walhere's men despite the obvious pain it caused him to move his taut, shiny red skin.

The pathway was just wide enough for one small wagon and several times they had had to squeeze past apologetic freeling as they descended into the next valley. The stillness of the ancient woodlands soon became as oppressive to the Geats as the heat of the day outside its leafy embrace. Wolves and bears were common here they knew and at one point they had surprised both themselves and a family of wild boar as they had stumbled unexpectedly upon a small glade. Perfectly hidden by their dappled coats the swine had suddenly emerged into the full glare of the sunlight as they had drawn abreast of the clearing. Beowulf had calmed his startled mount and prepared to bring his spear forward as the male boar had snorted and pawed the dusty forest floor in warning. Notoriously aggressive when surprised the boar could easily disembowel a horse or man with one swipe of its vicious tusks and they had remained motionless until the agitated boar had considered that its family was safely away and, with a final grunt, darted into the wald in their wake.

As Mockery, the great iron-grey wolf, chased the sun down towards the western hills the track emerged from the tree line and made its way, arrow straight, across to the ferry. Ahead the sky was transforming itself into a sheet of burnished bronze as the rays of the setting sun painted it in a brawl of sandy reds and pale oranges.

Beowulf shielded his eyes against the glare, squinting as he searched out the location of the hall which was their destination for that day. It was, he snorted, easy to find. The entire journey from Honovere to Theotmalli had passed in a succession of thickly wooded ridges and river filled valleys which ran up from the lands of the Francs in the South almost directly northwards to the Saxon interior. Wide roadways hugged the riverbanks and a steady procession of small trading craft plied these arteries of trade between the two German giants.

Naturally such obvious routes into each other's heartlands offered equally tempting routes for the passage of armies and the Saxons had fortified any natural choke points on the routes with a series of stoutly constructed halls and burgs. They were ideal locations to collect duty from the travelling merchants and the thegns who presided over these valleys had become wealthy and powerful men.

The hall crowned a natural hillock on the floodplain, reflecting a pale pinkish hue against the dark greens and darker shadows of the wald beyond as the late afternoon sun reflected from it's, typically Saxon, lime washed walls. A massive stockade skirted and enclosed the hall and the surrounding compound, the stout oak timbers weathered a pale silvery-grey by the actions of sun and rain.

A defensive ditch had been dug around the base of the mound and filled with water, no doubt tapped from the nearby river. High above it all, the golden dragon of Saxland twitched lazily in the soft summer breeze as a mass of rooks cawed noisily in the nearby treetops. It was an impressive hall.

A heat haze shimmered above the surface of the water meadow as they completed the last few yards of that day's journey and clattered on to the ferry. Beowulf noted again the independence of spirit shown by the ordinary Saxon freeling. In Geatland the ferry would have been put aside for his party's use but here, although the Saxons were not disrespectful in any way, they expected to share the passage with the obviously wealthy and important group of warriors.

It was a strange aspect of the Saxon people that each man seemed to believe that, although he was clearly not the equal in wealth or status of such men as himself and his companions, nevertheless they were no less worthy as those which would be considered at home to be their betters and it was a quality which, he had to admit, irked him.

Beowulf dismounted and stood at the rail of the raft, watching as the waters of the river tumbled past and trout rose to take insects from the air. Hrafn came and stood at his shoulder and indicated towards the fortress with a flick of his head.

"I wonder where they are off to, lord. They seem to be in a hurry."

Beowulf raised his eyes and looked across. Fully a score, heavily armed mounted warriors had emerged from the burg and were hastening down the doglegged path which led down from the great gated entrance. As they watched, the leading riders gained the water meadow and kicked in, surging forward onto the roadway which led south and sending a cloud of dust billowing in their wake.

Beowulf glanced across to Waldhere who was standing near the front of the ferry with one of his men.

"I hope that's not our welcoming party. They don't look to be in a friendly mood!"

Waldhere handed the reins of his horse to his companion and walked slowly across, watching the mounted riders as they swept down on the roadway as he did so. He shook his head, obviously deep in thought.

"I don't know for sure where they are going to but I have a good idea. They are heading south and there is only one danger in that direction and it is not our little party."

As if to confirm the Saxon thegn's conclusion the party of Saxons thundered past the western jetty which the ferry was now approaching, their long blue cloaks streaming in their wake, and hastened on to the South. Waldhere turned to Beowulf and his normally carefree mien had taken on a rather more serious aspect.

"They look as though they are heading down to bolster the warriors at the border. If you asked me for my opinion I would have to say that it can only mean that the Francs are finally reacting to your raid, lord."

*

"You cannot leave Beowulf. The runes were very clear. You must accompany the head of Grendel to the Irminsul and remain there for the duration of the midsummer ceremonies." They were sat in the hall of the Saxon thegn, Eadred, and Unferth was patiently explaining to Beowulf again that his duty lay in fulfilling the wishes of the Allfather and not with the army in far off Frisland.

Beowulf's immediate reaction to Waldhere's statement on the ferry had been to hurry on to the West and warn the forces at Dorestada that the Francs were massing against them. The Danish warloca was however slowly beginning to convince him otherwise. Unferth continued as they sat at their ale.

"You and I both know that Woden expects to be obeyed without question. Besides," he added, "how would it appear to the Saxons if you felt that the Geatish army could not survive without yourself and your two men. There is no way that you could reach Dorestada before the Francs even if you set off at first light. King Hygelac will have scouts and raiding parties scouring the lands to the South. He is an experienced warrior and he will not allow himself to become trapped in the town even if the Francs move against him in overwhelming force. Remain calm and your confidence in your people's abilities to cope with this threat will impress the Saxons."

Beowulf nodded thoughtfully as he listened. He had to admit to himself that there was more than a pinch of wisdom in the Dane's advice. He reached across and scooped up another piece of pork from the platter which lay before them and smiled as his decision was made.

"You are right. I have a duty to discharge for the Allfather before I worry about the Francs." He turned to Unferth and smiled. "I wish that I was there though," he managed to sigh through a mouthful of pork. "They will be having a great time."

NINE

Ealhstan threw a grin to his king as he casually raised his shield and Hygelac smiled warmly. He had known the man for nigh on twenty winters, ever since he had arrived at his hall as a scrawny boy. Hygelac had promised his father that he would make a warrior of the boy as he lay dying from a Swedish spear thrust to the belly and he had succeeded beyond his wildest dreams. A diet rich in meat and an outdoor life had worked wonders on the lad and Hygelac had looked on proudly the night he had danced with the wolf warrior and became a man. Tough and ever cheerful he had grown into a popular member of the king's war band. It would take more than a group of strange looking little men on children's ponies to faze the warrior he had become, Hygelac snorted happily.

A heartbeat later an arrowhead punched through the linden board and on into Ealhstan's eye socket. Hygelac gasped in disbelief and horror as the arrowhead exploded from the rear of his helm, a gruesome soup of blood, bone and brain tissue spattering his shocked friends.

Glancing back to the front he snatched his head to one side as another shaft whickered past, the fletching gently kissing his cheek as it flew past to embed itself deep in the shoulder of the man to his rear. Hygelac dropped instinctively into a crouch as the deadly darts snatched at man after man. Thankfully the strange riders were relatively few in number and Hygelac watched as the column broke to left and right as they snatched up another arrow from the large quiver which bounced at their knees.

The bowmen rode along the length of the Geat shield wall, marking their targets and loosing each shaft with deadly accuracy. For the men of the front ranks there was nowhere to hide from the wicked arrow storm and Hygelac watched, powerless, as some of his finest warriors tumbled forward like newly cut hay.

A voice came at his shoulder and he tore his gaze reluctantly away from the carnage developing to either side of his position to find that Wulf had moved instinctively in to protect his lord.

"They are Huns, lord," he explained. "Some of the Frisian warriors described them to us when we were down in Domburg that summer with Ealdorman Beowulf."

As they watched, the Hun column reached the ends of the shield wall and the leading riders started to trot back to the rear.

"Is that it?" Hygelac asked desperately, as he tried to comprehend the amount of damage which one pass had caused to their ranks. He was disappointed but not surprised to learn that the assault was far from over as Wulf grimly shook his head.

"They will form into two great counter-rotating circles and make several passes until their arrow supply is exhausted."

Hygelac looked at his hearth warrior in horror.

"We will all be dead by that time!"

Wulf shrugged.

"There are only two things that we can do to survive the power of those bows, lord. The obvious one is run away, and we are not going to do that are we!" he smiled encouragingly.

The first glimmer of hope since the Huns had arrived began to kindle in the king as he realised that Wulf may have an answer to the death-dealing Hunnic bowmen, but a quick glance back to the front confirmed that the leading elements had almost completed their circle and were approaching again. He looked back to Wulf and shot him a wry smile.

"Well, you either share this secret very quickly," he replied, "or else you will find yourself standing at the far end of the bridge alone!"

*

Time was short and although he had sent runners along the rear of the line to shout out the information which Wulf had shared with him Hygelac knew that most would never get to learn the secret, if that was what it was, of how to face down the terrible Hunnic bows before they too fell. He dropped his sturdy stabbing spear, his framea, and snatched up a handful of lighter angon from the place where they had been stacked to hand earlier. Hefting his shield Hygelac motioned to his companions to remain where they were and advanced alone onto the crest of the bridge.

Now in full view of all on the battlefield, the Geatish king planted his feet firmly and, splaying his arms, he raised his shield and spear as he cried a challenge to the onrushing Huns.

"I am Hygelac, son of Swerting, Woden born.

Your arrow storm holds no fear for us!

These are not Francs who stand in proud ranks before you now but Geats.

Ride in to your deaths little men!

Hygelac shifted lightly on the balls of his feet as the men in the shield wall roared their support. He had to get this right or he would resemble a giant hedgehog in moments. Moving his shield down across his body he left his head uncovered and pushed the board forward until it was one foot from his chest but moving freely and waited. Ahead, the first of the Huns nocked the arrow to his bowstring and raised the weapon as he came on. Hygelac concentrated hard as he watched the point of the arrow come up until it was aimed directly at his head. Fixing the bowman's lips with his stare, he waited for the man to take the breath which would indicate that he was about to release the arrow. He found that he really did need to blink but he dare not, it would in all probability cost him his life.

There!

As the Geatish king stared intently the lips of the nearest Hun pursed slightly. Hygelac knew that the bowman was gently expelling the air from his lungs as he prepared to release and the moment that he recognised movement from the bowstring he began to flick the wrist which held the shield upright. A heartbeat later the arrow thudded into the thick, leather covered board and punched through, inches from Hygelac's face.

Deflected by the upward, twisted movement, the shaft of the arrow lodged firmly in the body of the shield and hung there, impotently. Hygelac shifted his weight and concentrated on the following bowman, repeating his success as the frustrated Huns moved off to left and right. Satisfied that the men in the watching shield wall would learn from his example, Hygelac weighed the angon in his right hand, shifting it slightly as he sought the point of greatest balance. Instinctively aware of the moment he found it, Hygelac swatted away the following arrow and launched his counter attack.

The last attacker was wheeling his mount to the right as he reached down to snatch up another shaft from the quiver which bounced on his mount's fore quarter. A lightning fast glance to his left confirmed that the following Hun was not yet in a position to launch his attack , his bow still hanging down at his side as his horse trotted forward with its strange, shuffling gait.

Now!

Hygelac opened his body and, drawing back his arm, took aim on the Hun as he straightened up and concentrated on nocking his next arrow. The king's arm flew forward and the angon shivered across the intervening gap. As the Geats watched, a primeval sense of danger caused the rider to glance back at the figure of the king and his expression just had time to register a look of horror before the point of the angon transfixed his neck and emerged from the other side in a spray of blood. The man's hands clutched automatically at his neck as he slid slowly from view to the accompaniment of wild cheering from the watching Geats.

As Hygelac danced back to rejoin his companions on the near side of the bridge further cheers rose into the sultry afternoon air as Geatish angon began to fly out to take increasing numbers of Huns. Soon the warriors began to pair up, one man with a shield and one with a supply of angon. Working together the Geat casualties began to fall as those of the Huns rose steadily until, finally, the Hunnic riders broke their circles and retired back towards the Francish army at the foot of the meadow.

Hygelac removed his helm and swept the sweat soaked hair back from his face, blinking the stinging rivulets from his eyes. Thurgar grinned and held a cup of ale forward for his lord and Hygelac savoured the taste as it worked to refresh his parched throat. Finishing he belched and grinned at the crowd of smiling faces which surrounded him.

"Well, that was fun after all!" he exclaimed. "Who wants to go and look at a Hun?"

Hygelac led the men of his comitatus across the bridge and over to the nearest Hunnic corpse. The angon still pierced the bowman's neck as he lay sprawled upon the grass, and Hygelac indicated to Tofi that he turn him over onto his back with a flick of his head. Tofi ambled across and, with his knee planted firmly on the dead man's back, withdrew the angon with a soft sucking sound. They all crowded around as Tofi heaved the body over and snatched the man's fur hat from his head.

"If it wasn't for you Thurgar," Hygelac whistled, "I would have had to say that that is one of the most unusual looking bastards that I have ever seen!"

They all marvelled at the features on the first Hun which they had seen who was no longer actively trying to kill them. The high cheekbones and narrow eyes were familiar to them from the volva, the holy woman, at the temple back in Geatland. She shared many of the bowman's features, including the hair colour which was as black as any night. Wulf was the first to speak.

"He looks like the volva, Kaija." Tofi raised his eyebrow wickedly. "Well, not as beautiful!" he laughed. "Do you think that the Huns are from the North too?"

Hygelac shrugged.

"They could be. Not too far north though," he added. "That is where the frost giants live."

They all nodded at their king's wisdom as a loud roar carried up to them from the lower meadow. They looked across as one to see that the Francs were finally set in their divisions, a rippling wall of leather and steel which shimmered in the warm afternoon sun. Above each rank clouds of multicoloured standards stirred easily in the fitful breeze of a perfect summers day.

Hygelac glanced around his men, the men of his personal comitatus, the finest warriors on the field and found that they were almost to a man staring wistfully at the sky. He had seen the look many times before but this time, for the first time ever, he felt the same compunction to drink in the beauty of middle earth for the final time. It was as if men who realised that they were about pass from this world finally realised the beauty which had surrounded them throughout their lives while they had fretted and worried about trivial things. High above in the cobalt sky, a lone eagle circled slowly on ragged wings whilst in the treetops of the copse which anchored the Geat line to the east a murder of crows was gathering for the feast to come.

So, not all things here are beautiful. Bastards!

A passage from a long forgotten performance by a travelling *scop* came into his mind as he watched the dark birds bickering in the canopy.

The field flowed with the blood of warriors, from sun up in the morning when the glorious star gilded over the earth, till that noble creation sank to its seat.

There lay many a warrior by spears destroyed, northern men shot over shield, weary, war sated.

They left behind them to enjoy the corpses the dark coated one, the horny-beaked raven, and the dusky-coated one, the eagle white from behind, to partake of carrion, greedy war-hawk, and that grey animal the wolf in the forest.

Grimly Hygelac retrieved the angon which had been pulled from the neck of the Hunnic bowman and turned to go. It would make a fitting gesture to Woden, the Lord of Battle, if he used a weapon which was covered in the fresh blood of his enemy and dedicated the coming slain to the god with it. He did after all hope to feast in Woden's hall this night. He called to the others and started to walk back to the bridge.

"Come on boys, back we go. It looks as though we will have more guests to entertain soon."

Thurgar pulled a roguish grin.

"I hope that they have brought their own ale. I don't think that I laid enough in for that many guests, lord!"

They all gave a fatalistic laugh. None of them expected to see another day but, if they had been asked at any time in the past how they wished to end their days then fighting at the head of the army in a foreign land, shoulder to shoulder with their friends and king against impossible odds would have been most warriors ideal.

Thurgar squinted over to the West where the sun was beginning its long dip down to the world's rim. The ships of the fleet were just over there, safely coasting the waves of the German Sea, but in reality they may as well have been back in Geatland. Even if they *could* return they would most likely die alongside their trapped countrymen and the nation would fall as one of their neighbours, the Swedes, the Jutes or even the Heatho-Reams could gobble them up in their weakened state.

"Do you think that we will make it to the night, lord?" Thurgar asked as they regained their old position. Hygelac rubbed his beard as he thought. The time for soothing words of encouragement had long gone by, his men knew and deserved the truth, he recognised.

"It's difficult to say, Thurgar. The wolf does seem to chase the sun down earlier here but it is just past the solstice so..." he shrugged as he left the conclusion hanging in the air. In truth he doubted it, but it was possible.

"If Hromund can hold the lower bridge, maybe. If not..."

*

The ealdorman passed around the barrel of ale and waited patiently as his most experienced warriors drank their fill. The fighting had been heavy at the bridge all day as the Frisians, bent on revenge for their humiliation earlier in the summer and the depredations which they had suffered during the campaign, threw themselves repeatedly at Hromund's dwindling forces. Finally the barrel had completed its circle and Hromund hungrily gulped down the warm sticky liquid, closing his eyes in pleasure as the drink sated his raging thirst. Fighting was tiring and thirsty work and it felt as though they must have been fighting forever.

Hromund tossed the empty barrel to one side and looked gravely at the four dishevelled warriors gathered around him as he began.

"We can't hold here much longer, we all know that. None of us will see this night but the Allfather has given us the chance to decide the manner of our deaths. You four are the most experienced warriors here and I would value your opinions." He flicked his head in the direction of the man on his immediate right. Ulf had fought in the great battles against the Swedes outside Edet, the battle they came to know as Sorrow Hill. Later he had been one of the warriors of Beowulf's 'brotherhood' which had sailed to Dane Land and killed the monsters. Ulf still proudly wore the ring on his sword hilt which marked him out as one of that famous band and he shrugged and looked about him before turning back to Hromund with a wry smile.

"This looks as good a place as any, lord. If we pull the remaining men back to the bridge we can deny them passage to the king for as long as possible."

Hromund nodded thoughtfully as each man had their say. Finally they had all spoken and he looked around them and smiled.

"Well I agree with all of you, this *is* as good a place to die as any." He cast a look to either side as he spoke. The

Fris were preparing to launch boats filled with warriors about one hundred yards up and downstream of the bridge and he had to grudgingly respect the thinking behind the move. Their numbers were too few now to defend the entire stretch of the bank and to send men that far away from any means of support would only invite their annihilation and weaken the main position at the same time.

"Ulf, spoil the food in the wagons and get as much of the ale onto the bridge as you can. We may as well go singing!" he laughed. "When I give the word pull the remaining men in from the flanks and form a perimeter around this side of the bridge. At least we can force them to use boats to get their army across the river. It will delay them falling on the rear of the king's position as long as possible. It's the best we can do for them now."

Hromund moved forward and clasped each man's forearm in turn as a cry of alarm carried across from the warriors facing the town. They all looked across to see the flags and banners of the Frisians bobbing forward above the heads of the Geat defenders and Hromund's expression changed to one of steely determination. He heft his shield and turned towards the bridge.

"I think that it is time to go and forge our reputations."

TEN

Beowulf and Unferth reined in at the entrance to the tree lined valley and watched as the sea of people flooded around them. Beowulf chuckled and turned to the Danish warloca.

"We had best hurry or we shall have to file in with everyone else and may never reach the Irminsul. You have seen how bloody minded these Saxon freeling are if they think that their personal rights are being ignored."

Beowulf clicked his tongue and the mount responded immediately. Edging through the throng they made their way slowly down the wide sunlit pathway until a gentle turn to the left suddenly brought them within sight of the five great ridge stones which the Saxons called the 'God Wall.' Rising abruptly from the valley floor the sandy coloured columns climbed above the surrounding trees, towering, Beowulf estimated, to a height of one hundred feet or more.

Cola and Hrafn edged their horses past as they moved forward to clear a path for their lord, their size and obvious potential for sudden violence helping to curb the Saxons' unmistakable desire to protest. Once they had passed the bottleneck created by a pair of giant rune-carved columns which seemed to mark the boundary of the Osning the crowds fanned out and the going became easier.

They had left the hall of the Saxon thegn, Eadred, soon after first light that morning. Waldhere and his men had remained behind, helping to replace the men they had witnessed the previous day hastening to the Francish border, and a steady day's ride on good roads had brought them to the town of Theotmalli. As promised the town had been a maelstrom of activity and they had hurried on, following the crowds which were streaming along the road which led west into the Osning, for that night's midsummer celebrations.

After the many delays which they had experienced on their journey through the lands of the Saxons it was with some relief that Beowulf and Unferth could finally begin to relax, confident that they would reach the Irminsul in good time.

The wide grassy plain which led up to the god wall was bounded on the northern side by a large lake and they made their way across. The crowds had not reached this point yet and they dismounted and surveyed the area as the horses drank noisily.

Cola reluctantly hurried off to report their presence to the volur, the seeress who practised at the shrine, as they examined their surroundings. Ahead of them the vast majority of worshippers were heading for an ancient oak tree of enormous size which was obviously the Irminsul. Its age worn trunk towered above the surrounding trees, the gnarled features thrown into sharp relief by the deepening shadows cast upon it by the late afternoon sun.

To their surprise Cola returned soon after accompanied by a pair of Saxon warriors and whilst one escorted Unferth back to the holy wall the other apparently had been sent to help them understand the things which they would witness this midsummer's eve. Beowulf automatically appraised the man as he stepped forward to introduce himself. Tall and broad the warrior wore a fine shirt of leather lamellar armour, similar in cut to his own solid leather battle shirt. Unlike his own battle shirt however the design also allowed independent shoulder protectors to be attached to the main shirt, the inherent flexibility offered by the leather scales obviously being far less restrictive in use. Beneath this the man wore a short sleeved green linen under shirt hemmed in fine gold braid, whilst a wide silver buckled belt hung at his waist in the Saxon style.

"Welcome to the Osning, lord" The Saxon beamed. "My name is Brand. I have been instructed to accompany your party this evening to help you to understand the ceremonies which take place here."

Brand looked to be about seventeen or eighteen winters old and the gods had apparently decided to add a natural relaxed charm to the good looks and fine physique with which they had blessed the young man. He reminded Beowulf of the Swedish warrior, Alf, whom he had known during his time in Swede Land as an *eardwræcca,* an exile, several years ago. It augured well for the day.

Brand indicated to the horses with a flick of his head and a lazzi hastened across to lead them away as Beowulf introduced Cola and Hrafn to their guide.

"I was just admiring your war shirt, Brand. I have seen metal lamellar armour before but not leather. How do you rate its effectiveness?"

Brand twisted and flexed to illustrate the shirts best properties as they walked across to the great oak.

"I like to wear this during the summer, lord," he began. "Its much lighter than mail and keeps much cooler in the sun. I can wear just a linen under shirt and remain cool all day. As long as you keep the leather plates well greased it stays supple and water proof. Some men wear it during battle with a padded under shirt and say that it can be very effective but I have a mail byrnie and battle coat similar to your own for any serious battle play."

Beowulf nodded and remarked on the series of unusual scars which the man bore on his upper arm. They resembled a series of puncture wounds and he had not seen their like before. Brand glanced down and rolled up his sleeve to reveal an arc of old scars.

"Dog bites, lord, from a Francish war dog." Brand continued as he noticed Beowulf's surprised expression. "The Francs often release huge dogs as they charge at a shield wall and then, just as they hit, follow up with a volley of francisca throwing axes. It can be devastating if you are not expecting it..." Brand's voice trailed off as he realised that Beowulf and his men would be anxious for the fate of the army now that the Francs were apparently moving against them. "I am sure that your king can handle Francs, lord," he offered. "They covet our lands but we beat them off every time, despite their numbers. They have forsaken the gods for a weak god, the white god, and Saxnot will punish them for their disloyalty."

Beowulf seized on the chance to gain more recent information on the activities of the Francish army. He was desperate to return to the Geat army which he knew to be at Dorestada in Frisland but he had promised Woden that he would remain for this evenings ceremonies. Brand stopped and faced them as he shared all the information which had reached them in the Osning.

"Folk and traders coming up the River Lupia which runs west from here down to the Rin, say that King Theodoric has gathered a mighty army from amongst the Hetware, Bructeri and Cherusci and is moving against your king." Brand smiled at Beowulf's concerned expression and continued. "We know of the size and ability of the Geatish army in Frisland. We also know what it is like to face apparently overwhelming numbers of Francs but continually win the day nevertheless. The only way that the Francs will defeat your king is if he makes a mistake like dividing his forces which he would never do, would he lord."

*

As the sun moved down to clip the summit of the god wall Beowulf asked Brand to show them the Irminsul. They had travelled for over a month to reach this place and it was to be the centre of the midsummer festival the following sunrise. To their surprise Brand started to move away from the giant oak and began to lead them towards the pale columns of the ridge stones. Beowulf called after the Saxon as he strode away.

"I asked to see the Irminsul, Brand, not the god wall."

Brand turned back in confusion.

"Yes, lord, that is the Irminsul, the tall column in the centre. The volur, Albruna, has her cell at the summit. It is where you will rejoin the warloca and spend the last hours before dawn." Brand noticed the look of concern sweep across Beowulf's face. It was the first time that he heard that he would be present at the moment that Unferth delivered the head of Grendel to Woden and he had to admit to himself that the news was unwelcome. He had had enough contact with the gods over the years to be wary of their powers.

"Don't worry, lord," he chuckled happily. "You will still be with us in the morning!"

Several warriors were guarding the base of the steps which led up to the summit of the Irminsul and they nodded cheerfully as Brand explained the columns to them.

"The tall narrow column in the centre is the Irminsul, as I explained, lord. The volur lives there and never leaves. She receives all visitors in her cell there, it is where your friend the warloca is preparing to meet the Allfather as we speak. To the right the large stone represents Woden, the Allfather, and the smaller columns represent Saxnot, Tiwaz and Ing."

Beowulf stared up at the sheer columns of rock which towered above the valley floor. Steps had been cut into the column to the side of the Irminsul which curled, serpent like, to the summit. There, a narrow bridge connected the pathway to the Volur's cell. Beowulf shuddered as he imagined the rites which were being practised in the tiny room at this very moment and decided to move on.

"What is the giant oak then Brand if it is not the Irminsul? It seems to be the centre of attention."

"Thunor's oak?" Brand replied. "You will find out the power which lies there after dark," he added mysteriously. The space before the tree is kept free for men and women who wish Thunor to bless their union. It is a very special honour and they must show commitment by travelling to the tree on foot. Each year ten couples from each Gau, our name for the area ruled by an ealdorling, are invited to participate. It is a great honour for them."

Cola looked at Brand in amazement. The Englishman had always worshipped Thunor, as did most of his people, and he was keen to find out which form this 'power' would take.

"Will Thunor be here?" he asked in wonderment.

Brand smiled warmly as he noticed the hammer of Thunor which hung at Cola's neck for the first time. Fishing inside his shirt he pulled out a fine silver example of his own and kissed it reverently as he replied.

"Prepare to be astonished, Cola."

*

Beowulf and Hrafn hovered towards the rear of the huge mass of humanity which had gathered to share midsummer night with their gods. The last rays of the sun were finally dying to the West, directly behind the Irminsul, and an uncanny silence descended on the crowd as they waited for the gods to come amongst them. Thunor, the weather god, had earlier provided a fitting end to the old day as the horses had pulled the sun down to the rim of middle earth in a splash of reds and pinks. Now, as the sky finally transformed itself into a deep magenta the first stars began to wink into life like so many camp fires.

As the last rays were extinguished a rising note was sounded from the direction of the Irminsul and Beowulf watched as scores of brands flickered into life away to his left. Soon the multitude began to part as the procession moved forward into the space which had been reserved for them before the great oak.

They watched as the couples made their way forward beneath the torches and Beowulf recalled the explanation of the sights which he was now witnessing given to them earlier by their Saxon guide. The women were resplendent in long white gowns above their everyday clothing as a mark of their virtuous state. They would wear them until they became known to their new *bonda,* the man with whom she would share her life and raise her children. Most of the women wore summer flowers woven into their long unbound hair and Beowulf chuckled to himself as he remembered the scrambles which he had witnessed in the past for the flowers as they were tossed to the expectant crowd. The women would bind their hair at the conclusion of the ceremony and each carried a headdress in her right hand with which to cover her head when in public. It was the most obvious sign that a woman was no longer a maiden but a man's *wyf* and it was thought scandalous to be seen without it outside her own home.

The procession moved forward into the clearing and disappeared from sight as the crowds moved back together. The sky had darkened rapidly as they had watched the passage of the betrothed and, looking back the West, they found that the pillars of the god wall now stood out as solid darker forms against the sky, the misshapen teeth of a monstrous giant.

Beowulf snapped off another piece of crackling and chewed noisily as Hrafn trotted across to refill their ale cups. It was true, he reflected as he crunched away, the Germans really do know how to roast pork.

Brand had left them to watch the ceremonies from a raised area which had been constructed near the lake while he had taken his fellow Thunor worshipper, Cola, off to a place nearer the Thunor oak. What form the astonishing event would take was still unknown to him, but the Saxon thegns and their men who shared the platform with them seemed singularly disinterested at the moment as they plundered the special celebratory ale which the volur's helpers had apparently been brewing for months beforehand. Wagons had deposited barrels of the special ale amongst the crowd and they had been drinking steadily since late afternoon. The ale carried a tang which Beowulf thought that he recognised from long ago, but he could not quite place where he had tasted it before. It was unusual in that it looked like the *laager* which he had drunk in Frisland, but tasted more like the dark ale he knew from home. The Saxons called it wit bier, white beer, and apparently the celebratory drink had been prepared using plants and grains known only to the volur and her helpers.

Hrafn returned with the beer as a great cry arose from the direction of the oak. Looking across they could just make out the shadowy images of flowers as they sailed over the torches and disappeared back into the gloom.

"Looks like that is all over, lord. Maybe we will find out what this great thing will be now?"

As if in reply to the big Swede's statement a buzz ran through the crowd as a fire flickered into life high on the god wall. In moments the flames had taken a firm hold and Beowulf and Hrafn watched as they roared hungrily skywards beneath a boiling mantle of dark grey smoke.

The setting of the fire was obviously a signal and the fellow warriors on the platform replaced their cups and moved to the edge nearest the crowd. An expectant hush descended over the bowl of the clearing as thousands of people seemed to hold their breath as they awaited the appearance of their god.

Beowulf was reminded of the great disablot he had attended at Uppsala. That day the god Frey had taken possession of the Swedish King Ongentheow and moved amongst his people. It had been an awe inspiring event which would remain in Beowulf's mind always and he searched the shadows as he sought out any signs that Thunor had likewise come amongst the Saxons.

Hrafn gently touched his arm and he looked back to the front as a soft gasp escaped from the lips of the crowd. Beowulf squinted as his eyes tried to pierce the gloom.

"No, lord," Hrafn gasped at his side. "Not in the crowd; Look at the tree!"

Beowulf raised his head and looked across at the massive form of the Thunor oak. The flames from the pyre were roaring high into the inky blackness and the light which they threw out was dancing and flickering along the irregular fringe of the tree line. As his eyes alighted on the massive oak Beowulf too let out an involuntary gasp. The knots and limbs of the ancient tree were slowly beginning to take the form of a giant man.

To his right the Saxon thegns and their men were smiling warmly as their god took shape before them and the northerners watched in wonderment as the head and arms of the giant began to move. As the crowd began to softly chant, Thunor appeared to look down on the throng of worshippers at his feet. Slowly he reached forward with his arms and Beowulf saw that he was gripping his mighty hammer, crusher, which he seemed to hold over the gathering.

The firelight washed over the god, illuminating his features as he appeared to smile at his devotees. Beowulf suddenly became aware that the men nearest him were drawing back respectfully as the figure of a woman appeared at his side and he tore his gaze away from the fantastic events before him and glanced down.

Before him stood a tall young woman dressed in the white robes of the volur. Her long, hazel coloured hair, fell in sweeps to her waist and the beauty of her upturned face was only sullied by the almost mocking coldness which lived in her eyes. She smiled thinly and indicated towards the god wall.

"Beowulf, you are to follow me," she ordered. "It is time for you to prepare."

*

The Geat was almost there and he urged his horse forward as he tried desperately to beat the intercepting Fris riders to the crossroads. It was only one hundred yards ahead of him now and he was beginning to think that he might escape after all. He was the last member left alive from the foraging party which his thegn had sent out several days before, unaware that an advance party of the Frisian army was bearing down on Dorestada under the leadership of their young king, Ida.

The Geat cursed the roads in this gods forsaken place for the hundredth time that day. The land was so wet and waterlogged that travel was restricted to a series of man made ridges which crisscrossed the land. He had had to continually double back on himself as he tried to escape the Fris war band which had suddenly fallen on them as they had been busy chasing pigs around a muddy pen.

Luckily he had been searching the hall for food when the Frisian warriors had arrived unexpectedly and he had watched in horror as they had slit his companions bellies open and laughed as the pigs set to, eating the Geats innards which had slithered to the ground before their terror stricken eyes.

As he had watched from his hiding place the Frisian lord had arrived and finished off his friends, to the obvious disappointment of one malevolent looking bastard, chastising the man for his bestiality.

Seizing his chance he had slipped out of the hall and run to his mount, speeding south just as the cry of alarm sounded from the hall.

The horse clattered between the small halls which had grown up around the crossroads and the Geat breathed a small sigh of relief as he glanced back to see that the pursuing Fris were still fifty yards to the rear.

Dayraven watched the shadow of the Geat horseman move swiftly along the side of the building opposite him and began to swing. With perfect judgement he stepped from the shadows and brought his blade crashing down on the neck of the galloping horse. Practically beheaded by the savage blow the horse ran on for a few steps before it crashed to the roadway in a welter of flying legs, thick jets of arterial blood pumping on before it. His men clattered to a halt beside him on blown horses, their foam flecked flanks heaving like monstrous bellows. The leading rider reined in and smiled at the leader of his war band as he surveyed the carnage on the road.

"He could really ride, lord!"

Dayraven nodded and walked across to the place where the injured and dazed Geat was attempting to rise to his feet.

"Well, he has one more ride to take. Straight to Hel's dank hall!"

ELEVEN

Hygelac watched, exasperated, as the great mass of the Francs drew to a halt one hundred yards before the river. He was beginning to grow very weary of the piecemeal tactics which their leader was employing against them. He had accepted that he was to die this day and, to his surprise, the acknowledgement had lightened his mood considerably. Shorn of responsibility for his own wyrd and that of others, he was beginning to savor his last few hours on middle earth and was concentrating now on the manner which his death would take. Even outnumbered twenty to one the price would be high to gain the bones of a king of Geats he promised himself. He had a plan and, if even the remotest opportunity to carry it out presented itself to him, he would seize it eagerly.

The Geats looked on as the Francish line opened up to admit a series of wagons into the space between the armies. The wagons drew to a halt fifty yards south of the river and the horses were uncoupled and led back to the rear as men ran forward to surround the wagons with woven barriers.

Hygelac called across to Wulf as the men on the wagon began to assemble a series of wooden objects.

"Wulf, I don't suppose that your Frisian friend told you what they might be doing now, did he?"

The hearth warrior looked nervously across and Hygelac felt a chill run down his spine which was completely at odds with the warmth of the day. Wulf pursed his lips anxiously as he studied the strange contraptions.

"I am not sure, lord," he began to answer before pausing, obviously deep in thought. "I seem to remember him describing something called a ballista which the Romans used to open up shield walls. It looses off a great bolt which scythes through groups of densely packed men and opens their formation up to the attackers." A frown creased Wulf's brow as he tried to remember further details. "I am sorry, lord, that is all I can think of," he finally admitted, adding sheepishly, "we had rather a lot to drink that night. Ale and memory never were good companions!"

A rumble of laughter came from the group as Hygelac called back to the men he had assigned as runners. They hastened forward as the warriors nervously watched the Francish preparations. Until Wulf had spoken they had imagined a glorious death, finally falling, sword in hand, surrounded by the bodies of their enemies. To be smashed to bloody pulp from a distance seemed to be a dishonourable, almost cowardly way to die. The first man pushed his way through to the king and listened attentively.

"Race along the rear of the line and tell the men that we think that those wagons will unleash giant bolts at them.

Tell them to wait until the instant that the bolt is released and then drop to the earth. We still have the advantage of the rising ground and earth banks before us so they should pass directly over their heads." He indicated that the messengers should go with a flick of his head. "Be quick about it!"

Hygelac glanced back at the fiend and let out a sigh of disappointment. He had toyed with the idea of leading a quick dash towards the nearest of these ballista, killing the crews and at least damaging the things before help could arrive, but as he watched the Francs were moving forward to take up positions just behind the wagons. He doubted that they were acting merely in support, they were preparing to attack. He risked a glance along the line of his own forces and noticed the men in the front row cocking their heads to the rear as they listened to the shouted advice from the messengers. He could tell how far the men had moved along the line by following the reactions of those in the front ranks and he noted with satisfaction that very few, if any, of the men would now be surprised by this new weapon which it would seem was about to be unleashed upon them.

A shouted command carried from the enemy and Hygelac looked back to the front just in time to see the willow panel which had shielded the ballista fall forward. A series of loud *thwacks* punctured the air as the first of the bolts were released against them and the king instinctively fell to the floor amidst a jumble of bodies. A heartbeat later Hygelac felt the air move above him as the heavy bolt passed inches from his head and disappeared in a blur. To either side of him screams rent the air from those who had been either too slow to fall to the ground or had let their concentration wander momentarily and paid the blood price in death or mutilation.

As Hygelac prepared to lever himself back to his feet he realised that he was laying face to face with Wulf. The warrior grinned mischievously at his king and said simply.

"Boo!"

Wulf's calm, ridiculously childlike response to imminent death, caused the men of his comitatus to howl with laughter and Hygelac lay amongst them as helpless as any. As another bolt thundered above them Hygelac fervently hoped that the sound was carrying down to the ballista crews.

It would take more than Roman relics to break the spirit of this shield wall!

*

Hromund gritted his teeth and pushed back with all of his strength. The Frisians had managed to batter them back almost to the centre of the bridge by sheer weight of numbers. If they could heave the small Geatish force over the lip which marked the centre of the bridge they would prevail, the Geats would collapse as the slippery roadway fell away beneath them, and the army of the Fris could flood across and fall on the undefended rear of the main Geatish army.

He turned his head to one side and grimaced at his right hand man as the Fris pushed again.

"It's looking bad Ulf. This could be it," he managed to grunt through gritted teeth.

Ulf managed a small smile as he made what he thought would be his last quip in this world.

"I'll say, lord. They have nearly reached the ale barrels!"

Despite the desperate situation Hromund snorted at the comment before his expression changed to one of hope. He called out to the man he knew was immediately behind him above the snarls and grunts of scores of heaving warriors.

"Harold, you guarded the ale supplies. How many ale barrels do we have in total?"

Harold clearly thought that he had misheard his lord as he continued to throw his weight behind the shield wall.

"Lord?"

"You heard me, how many?" Hromund snapped back.

Harold quickly calculated as the Frisians surged forward, sensing that victory was within their grasp.

"About half a dozen full barrels and nine... or ten... empty ones, lord," he answered dutifully.

"Good," Hromund grunted. "This is what I want you to do."

Ulf grinned as Hromund explained his plan to Harold who immediately retired to the rear to organise the attack. Risking a glance to his left Hromund saw that he may have left it too late as another push by the warriors before them brought the front lines level with the high point of the bridge. One more push would be enough but, just as he began to despair, Harold screamed in his ear.

"All set, lord!"

"Do it!" Hromund snapped desperately as he braced himself to leap into any gaps which opened up before him.

He was dimly aware of the shadows cast by the empty barrels as they sailed over his head to fall deep within the

Frisian ranks and he gripped the hilt of his sword tighter as he waited for the chaos to escalate. Despite the noise of the attack Hromund clearly heard the grunts of the men behind him as they hoist one of their number to waist height on a shield. The warrior heaved the full barrel of ale onto the heads of the Frisian front ranks and the effect was immediate and devastating.

The man directly before him disappeared in an instant as the barrels rained down. Hromund and Ulf crashed into the gaps left by the fallen men and pushed deep within the enemy ranks. Normally they would have fanned out as they broke an enemy shield wall, widening the breach, but here, in the confines of the bridge, the object was even simpler. Hromund knew that they must regain control of the roadway to stand any chance of holding off the multitude gathered before them and he moved forward savagely as the Frisians, so certain of victory only moments before, began to break and scramble away as confusion and panic set in. With a roar which belied their numbers the Geats swept forward, slashing and stabbing at any Frisian within reach.

A hand clasped at Hromund's leg and, glancing down he noticed a Frisian warrior moving across to stab upward with a short seax. The ealdorman's sword flashed down to take the man in the throat, his lifeblood pulsing across the roadway. To his right Ulf had transfixed a warrior on the point of his framea and was drawing his own seax with a sweep of his arm. As Hromund moved forward he saw the big Geat thrust his shield into the face of the man before him and plunge the seax into his exposed side.

The Frisian line was in complete disarray now and Hromund and Ulf pushed over towards the bridge parapets as the Geat warriors poured through between them. As the enemy continued to fall back in confusion Hromund risked a glance over towards the far side of the river and was surprised to see that a small knot of mounted Fris were watching the fight from the bank. As he watched, intrigued, one warrior in a magnificent helm rode slowly forward beneath a large raven banner and beckoned to the man who appeared to be leading the Frisian forces assaulting the bridge. The man hurried across and stood listening intently, clearly receiving orders. Hromund flicked a look back at the fighting on the bridge. They had retaken half of the roadway on the northern side now. He would have to call a halt and consolidate their position before they weakened the southern side, there were just too few of them left to hold the entire span of the bridge, he knew.

Gazing back towards the far bank Hromund watched as the man returned to the Frisian warriors with his instructions and immediately the enemy retreated to the far bank and reformed their shield wall at the entrance to the bridge. A voice spoke at his shoulder and he turned to see that Ulf had joined him. "That was inspired thinking, lord," Ulf smiled, "and we recovered the barrels!" He glanced across and indicated the figure on horseback with a flick of his head. "He's a big bastard. Who do you think that he is, their king?"

Hromund shrugged apathetically.

"He could be. He certainly looks the part." Ahead of them the majority of the Frisian warriors had left the position at the foot of the bridge and were busily jogging along the far bank towards the crossing points. Hromund looked up and saw that the Fris had stopped rowing

117

individual parties of warriors across and had all but completed the task of securing a succession of boats together to form a pontoon. Very soon the army would be able to cross in numbers and outflank them. It no longer mattered that they were denied use of the bridge and the leader opposite had obviously decided to leave just enough warriors at the bridge to keep the Geats there from escaping.

As the mounted group broke up and followed on to the crossing points the leading warrior amongst them nodded curtly towards Hromund in recognition of the Geats' spirited defence and, pulling on the reins, made to join the others. As he did so a breath of wind blew off the river and a raven's wing, huge and black, lifted and fell as if to bid them farewell from the *walu*, the crest, on the man's helm.

Hromund and Ulf watched as the last boat was wedged alongside to complete the pontoon crossing and the Fris began to flood across.

The ealdorman punched Ulf on the arm and indicated the barrels of ale which still lay where they had fallen at the beginning of the attack.

"We may as well break open a few of those, it looks as though our fighting is over for now."

Ulf called across to Harold to organise it as Hromund added... "and roll a couple down to our Frisian friends. We *should* pay the toll, we *are* on their bridge after all."

*

The messenger slipped from his mount and tore across to the place where the white boar standard of Geatland curled defiantly in the soft summer breeze. Pushing through the crowd of warriors he approached the king and bowed his head as he waited for permission to speak. Hygelac turned to the man with a smile of resignation. Realistically, he knew, he could only be bringing a last warning from his old friend that they were about to be overrun and that he would soon be faced with a fight on two fronts.

"Don't tell me," he said. "Hromund has routed the Frisians and is coming across to help us finish off the Francs."

The men of his comitatus laughed at the grim humour of their lord. None of them were under any illusions that the end was edging a little closer for them all with every heartbeat. They could practically feel the presence of the *wælcyrge*, Woden's battle maidens, and each man now only longed for the chance to die well in the eyes of his friends and gain their place in the hall of the battle-slain.

The messenger, less accustomed to the acerbic wit of his king, stared in blank faced bemusement as the warriors' laughter washed around him. Finally he decided that he would relay his message whatever the king had meant by his remark.

"Ealdorman Hromund reports that the Frisians are beginning to outflank his position and that he cannot delay them much longer." A note of wariness crept into the messenger's voice as he continued. He obviously did not understand the last part of the message and was unsure whether he was about to offend his king. "He says that he has spent all day kicking the bear in the arse and it's about time that you had a go, lord."

Taken unawares by his friend's reference to their childhood adventure on the Troll's Hat, Hygelac breathed in deeply as he fought to keep his composure. He nodded that he understood and patted the man on the shoulder.

"Join your king in his last fight. Fight well and we may all be supping in a better place before Hater, grim wolf, chases the moon into the evening sky."

Hygelac glanced back across to the mass of Francs arrayed to his front. Grouped in their divisions a long bow shot distant, the Francs were becoming visibly more agitated as the time for their long delayed final assault grew nearer. The sun was lowering to the West now in a bone-fire of amber and crimson and the heat had finally come off the day. It was a good time for the assault, he knew, and it could not now be long delayed.

Frustrated in their attempts to smash the Geat shield wall by the lie of the land and the quick thinking of the Geat king, the Francish ballista had been pulled down the slight incline to the west of the bridge and repositioned as a more compact group. Hygelac knew that it could only mean that the Francs were going to cross the river down stream and outflank his shield wall but in truth he did not have the numbers to counter the threat and the Francish leader knew it. He dare not leave the relative safety of the higher ground as he would lose possession of not only bridge but the protection of the wood to his left. Isolated in the open, the Geats would be quickly overwhelmed as the Francs and Fris swarmed around them.

As if to confirm his fears Thurgar at his side called out and pointed downstream. Hygelac glanced across as the upright prows of several boats were rowed into view. As they watched, the leading boat grounded itself alongside the southern bank as the following boat drew up alongside it. Crewmen immediately began to lash the boats together as they came up and in a short space of time the pontoon was half way across the small river channel.

As the elements on the far end of the Francish force began to move off in the direction of the crossing, mounted warriors began to arrive at the nearside bank from Hygelac's rear. For a brief moment his heart leapt as he assumed that they were mounted elements sent by Hromund to contend the crossing but the sight of the banner which came into view only confirmed what he realised on reflection must be the truth. Led by a bear of a man the riders gathered together on the lower field beneath the sea eagle of Frisland, screening the point at which the Francs would cross from any possible counter attack by the Geatish force.

A murmur rippled along the Geat shield wall as the warriors realised that they now had to contend with an imminent attack on three sides. Hygelac knew that it was time to move his position to the place he had chosen for his death-fight and he turned to Thurgar at his side and clasped his forearm in the warrior fashion.

"I am going to pull the wings in and consolidate our position. I want you to deny them the bridge for as long as you can, then meet me in valhall," he smiled fatalistically. The king exchanged a last look with his hearth companion, the man he had known for a score years or more and, patting him affectionately on the shoulder, turned to go. "Until later then," he said as he began to move to the rear.

Thurgar nodded and watched him leave.

"Until later, lord."

TWELVE

Beowulf climbed the last of the steps and paused at the narrow bridge which led across to the summit of the Irminsul. Ahead he could see the tip of the cell in which he knew the Saxon volur and the Danish warloca were waiting for him to help fulfil the wishes of the Allfather and carry the head of the Grendel to him in valhall. The cell looked to be very small and he hoped that he would be able to fit his fully armoured body into the tight space. He had obviously dressed for war to meet the battle god and he began to feel that he may have made a mistake.

Backlit by the huge balefire which roared and crackled atop the adjoining pillar Beowulf cast a giant shadow across the Irminsul as he made his way reluctantly across. As he grew nearer he became aware of a slight scent in the atmosphere and the rhythmic beating of a drum carried to him in snatches on the still warm air

Ducking inside the chamber he was met by a scene which reminded him of the last time that he had met the god. The cell had been carved from the living rock and measured approximately twelve feet by six. In the centre of the room there was a long rectangular altar stone at the head of which a circular hole about the size of a man's fist had been cut into the eastern wall. Ahead of him on the left the volur sat on a raised platform, dressed completely in white and with her hair fashioned into a series of spikes with what Beowulf suspected was lime wash. A small drum lay before her which she was slowly beating in time. To one side of the volur a small fire crackled and flared as the holy woman added a handful of small seeds which Beowulf knew to be henbane. The seeds burned brightly and gave off the choking white smoke which swirled in the air about them.

Unferth stepped forward and led Beowulf into the inner reaches of the cell as he fought to control his breathing in the reeking fug which filled the cell. As expected, the Dane had dressed in his raven garments complete with beaked hood and, although Beowulf had both already seen the warloca in the costume and had fully expected to see the holy man in the costume on this night, he was nevertheless appalled at the sight in the present surroundings.

The warloca handed Beowulf a shallow bowl containing a thin gruel he suspected was seith-soup and he obediently spooned the mixture as they watched. He had eaten the soup before, the last time that he had met Woden, and he knew that he would soon be going on a spirit journey. The last one that he undertaken had been a pleasant, even joyful, occasion and he hoped that this would be equally enjoyable.

Beowulf was led to a small shelf which had been cut into the side of the wall and he rested there as the effects of the gruel began to add to the feelings of elation which the wit beer had seemed to produce in those who drank it.

As Unferth and Albruna chanted rhythmically Beowulf felt himself slipping in and out of consciousness as a series of visions flitted in and out of his mind like bats in the night. In one particularly vivid vision he found that he had become an eagle soaring above a large field. A small army was trapped between two rivers whilst an enormous host moved against them from all directions.

A light flickered ahead of him before it burst suddenly into his vision and he was dimly aware that it must be the return of the sun on midsummers morning. The hole in the end of the chamber he knew faced directly eastwards into the rising sun, and he watched in detachment as the shadow cast by the volur appeared to grow and completely envelop the spread-eagled form of the warloca which lay upon the altar.

The clatter of beating of wings suddenly caused him to start and a dark form entered the cell. Albruna knelt and handed up the grotesque head of the Grendel and the formless shadow gathered it in, swathing it in its cloak. Reaching across the amorphous shape scooped up the inert form of Unferth with incredible ease and appeared to merge with the darkest reaches of the cell as the shadows finally won their battle with his consciousness and crept forward to swallow Beowulf.

*

Beowulf, Cola and Hrafn boarded the boat which would carry them north to Dorestada along the waters of the mighty River Rin. Stowing their belongings in the open area amidships they glanced across and waved a grateful farewell to Brand as he gathered up the reins of the horses which had borne them west and trotted back to the nearby town. A cry came from the boat master and a crewman unhooked the hawser from the thick oak mooring post and tossed it aboard, following on a heartbeat later. Pushing off from the quayside the boat wallowed in deeper water as the oars slid proud of the hull and, as they began to rise and fall in unison, pointed her short stubby prow out into the waterway.

It had been three days since Beowulf had awoken, disorientated and nauseous, in a small hall at the base of the god wall. Disturbing images of the events of the previous dawn had returned to him in snippets during the course of the day but he had pushed them aside as he concentrated his efforts on regaining the army in far off Frisland. Cola had returned full of wonder at the sights which he had witnessed at Thunor's oak and, his faith reaffirmed by the experience, he too was keen to return to the Geat army and join them in the fight against those who had so recently abandoned the true gods.

Despite their protestations Beowulf had insisted that he had been well enough to travel and they had immediately joined the steady trickle of people on the road which led away from the Osning. Albruna, the volur, had apparently instructed Brand that he remain with the Geats until they reached the border of Saxland and Beowulf had been overjoyed when the man had reappeared that morning leading fresh horses and remounts. Combined with his knowledge of the area it would ensure that the Geat party would rejoin the army of Hygelac at the earliest opportunity.

Within the hour the forest track which led up to the god wall had deposited them onto the Roman Road which stretched away to the West, directly down to the River Rin. Brand had explained that, '*the road follows the course of the River Lupia which has its source in the Osning at a spring which the locals call 'Woden's eye.' The area from here to the Rin was a main route for the Roman army into the wald when they still had hopes of adding our lands to their empire.*'

During the days of hard riding which it had taken to reach the confluence of the rivers the Geats had marvelled at the remains which the army of Rome had left to litter the Saxon landscape. Where the Lupia ran alongside the road the remains of great store houses hugged the banks, the depositories for the vast amounts of foodstuffs and other supplies which, he knew from his own experience, an army whether on campaign or not, required each and every day. At regular intervals the Romans had built a series of fortified places which the Geats knew were called castrum. They had seen an example on the coast of Britannia when they had gone to kill the pirate known as *Blaecce shucca,* and although these castrum were not as commanding as the one which Grimma, his English friend had called Dommoc, they were still objects of wonder to men more used to dark halls built of timber and lime.

The Saxon boat pulled out into midstream and with a push of the big steer board the boat master pointed her nose downstream. Beowulf stared across at the town of Santen on the opposite, Francish, bank of the river as the crew settled into a steady rhythm. He had paid the owner handsomely in good silver to ensure that they reached Dorestada at the earliest opportunity. Beowulf knew that the army of King Theodoric was moving against the army of his king and kinsman and he was eager not to miss the upcoming battle. It would be, he knew, a great victory for his people, perhaps the greatest, and he was desperate to add another glorious episode to the tale of his life.

Beowulf, Cola and Hrafn stared across and drank in the sights of the town of Santen as the river swept them by. Perched on twin hills, the old and new castrum of Santen had been the place where the great warrior Sigurd the dragon slayer had lived out his days. The great town still lay enclosed within its protective ring of stone and they marvelled at the upper levels of colonnaded temples and public buildings, glimpsed above the high curtain walls.

As the day wore on and the heat abated, the walls and rooftops of Santen grew increasingly indistinct until they disappeared completely in the haze. Ahead of them the Rin grew ever wider as it began to make its turn to the West towards the sea and the Geats began to relax as the end of their journey came a little closer with every pull of the oars.

Despite the richness of the land to both sides of the river, Beowulf recognised the familiar signs of a border area everywhere that he looked. Small settlements and single farmsteads had replaced the grand castrum and ordered towns constructed centuries before by the great power in the South. He was traversing the very line which marked the frontier between Christian Francland and their great rival, Saxland, still a bastion of the older, true gods, and the sense of enmity was almost palpable as the rival giants glowered at one another across the watery waste which was the mighty Rin.

As the day slowly receded in a wash of scarlet and pink the boat master handed the big steering blade to a crew member and moved forward to join them. Bebba smiled warmly as he settled himself on a swirl of ropes and took a pull from his ale skin.

"We will be reaching the point where the river divides into two channels soon, lord." The man tensed and belched as the beer worked its way down before continuing. "The Rin travels straight on, west to Dorestada while the left fork becomes the River Woh as it meanders off towards the sea. There is a small settlement a few miles along the Rin which we should make before dark. It's not much of a place," he shrugged apologetically, "the thegn lives a score or more miles inland, but we would find a roof for the night if that is your wish."

Beowulf pondered his choice for a moment as he gazed out at the fast flowing waters. It had been a week or more since he had enjoyed a relaxed night under the shelter of a roof but as much as the thought appealed to him he knew that towns were probably best avoided. Apart from the fact that they all seemed to smell of animals and their shit, he felt comfortable on board the boat. The gods knew what the situation was on land with the Francs apparently on the move and he knew that they would be far safer on board. He unstopped his own skin of Saxon beer and took a swig.

"How close are we to Frisland, Bebba?"

The Saxon stroked his beard and glanced downriver as he thought.

"Five...six miles, there is a channel known as Drusus' Fossa connecting the Rin to the River Isla which marks the border there. There is a small settlement near the fossa called Arnheim after the number of eagles which live in the hills and woods around there."

Beowulf nodded and studied the distant bank of Francland as he deliberated. In the mad rush to rejoin the army he had not had time to think through any potential problems which they may encounter on the journey. The day spent idle on Bebba's boat had provided him with plenty of time for reflection and he had grown increasingly uneasy. The Saxon ealdorling, Aldwulf, had told him that the army of the Fris had been easily defeated by Hygelac and the Geats but that had been many weeks ago. Even the vague warning that the army of King Theodoric was finally responding to the raid was old news by now. In fact, he realised uneasily, he knew next to nothing about the current situation. He decided that they would moor the boat on the Saxon side of the river for the night as he decided what his next move would be. He desperately needed more information before he blundered blindly forward but how could he get it?

*

Beowulf started awake as a hand was laid gently on his shoulder. Hrafn leaned forward and spoke softly in the dark.

"Lord. You need to see this."

Beowulf levered himself upright and peered across to the place which the Swede was indicating. A line of torches were just flickering into life downstream, their pale yellow light reflecting dully from the greasy surface of the river. He glanced to one side as Bebba lowered himself carefully down beside them.

"We have got company, lord."

Beowulf nodded.

"So I see. Is this usual on the river, they are not fishermen or traders?" he suggested hopefully.

Even by the pale light of the moon Beowulf could see the boat master pull a wry smile.

"No, they are warriors, lord." He snorted. "Look at the height of the stem posts, they are small dracca. The big question is, whose side are they on."

"Francs?" Beowulf offered, hoping that he was wrong.

Bebba grimaced and shook his head.

"They shouldn't be, not from that direction, lord. They should be our boats on this stretch of the Rin but I don't see why they would be behaving like that." He paused and bit his lip nervously as he thought. Finally Bebba shrugged and glanced back to Beowulf.

"Unless they belong to your lot, lord, they can only be Frisians. They could have come down the Isla and used the fossa to outflank your army, or.." he began before tailing off, reluctant to put his thoughts into words. Beowulf completed them for him. "Or things could be a lot more different at Dorestada than we were led to believe."

Bebba nodded grimly and flicked a look back at the mystery boats.

"Well, it would seem that we will know for sure soon, they are still coming on."

Beowulf raised his head above the wale and looked downstream. The boats had left the northern channel and were beginning to fan out across the main watercourse. They were clearly searching for something or someone and it must be important to them to continue their search during the hours of darkness. As they watched, the light from the nearest boat picked them out from the shadows and the prow of the boat edged gently towards them. Bebba cursed as the outline of the boat, which he was now confident *were* Frisian, swung until it was clearly pointed directly at them.

"Shit! I hoped that they were going to pass us by," he cursed.

Beowulf glanced across to Hrafn and Cola. As expected Hrafn had already woken Cola and they had been following the conversation. He nodded to them and they made to arm without a word. Beowulf turned back to Bebba as he began to tighten his battle shirt.

"How many men do you think are on that boat, Bebba?"

The Saxon boat master answered immediately.

"I have seen them before. They are only small boats designed for river use, lord. They carry a steersman and a dozen oarsmen, six each side."

Beowulf's face lit up and he beamed at Cola and Hrafn who were grinning wolfishly.

"A dozen men!" he breathed delightedly as he unsheathed his gladius, Troll Killer.

Bebba looked horrified.

"You are not thinking of taking them on, lord!" he gasped.

The three Geats nodded enthusiastically in reply. Bebba cast a quick look back at the approaching boat. The upright prow of the Frisian vessel was beginning to come around, back to the east as the steersman leaned into the big paddle blade and took the way off the boat. In moments they would come within hailing distance and Beowulf saw the concern etched on Bebba's face as he turned back and pleaded with him.

"If you attack these men you will kill them all, I have no doubt about that, lord. But what will happen then?"

Beowulf shrugged. He would deal with the consequences as they occurred, it was the warrior's way. Bebba lowered his voice as the Frisians crept closer. The Saxon crew were now being woken by their companions on watch and a small knot of worried men were gathering to hear the conversation between the two leaders. Bebba fixed Beowulf with a stare and asked a question, slowly and deliberately.

"Do you trust me, lord?"

Beowulf found that he was nodding without giving the matter any thought. He had always prided himself on his ability to judge a man's character and he had taken an instant liking to the man when Brand had introduced them that morning. Bebba continued.

"If you kill those men it will bring the others down on us before we can escape. Even if you manage to kill the entire force you will alert the Frisians that there is a Geat force upstream when they fail to return. Sit with your back to them, lord, and I will find out what information that I can from them. We may as well turn this to our advantage if we can."

Before Beowulf had a chance to reply a voice carried across the water from the now stationary Frisian boat. Beowulf slid across to the side of the boat and listened as Bebba hopped back onto the steering platform.

"Who are you?"

Beowulf silently slid his gladius from its scabbard and placed it across his lap, running his gaze slowly across the nervous looking crew members as he did so. The threat was clear, one word out of place and they would be the first to die. To his right he heard Bebba hawk and spit into the water as he answered the Frisian challenge.

"I am a Saxon in Saxon waters. Who in Hel's saggy tits are you?"

Beowulf smiled to himself as the Frisian chose to ignore the tone of Bebba's reply and tried a different tack. He was beginning to become fonder of the Saxon sense of self worth. It was not, as he had first thought, a threat to the established social order but the glue which bound the people together. It was in fact the trait shared by the folk of the individual tribes which identified the Saxons as a nation.

"We are Frisian warriors. We are looking for Geat pirates. Have you seen any?"

Bebba shrugged and called to the crew members who had all now collected amidships to hear the verbal duel.

"Have we seen any Geat pirates lads?"

It was all that Beowulf and his companions could do not join in the laughter as one of the crew shot back; "What do they look like, Bebba?"

The Saxon boat master turned back to the Frisian warrior and held his arms wide in an apologetic gesture.

"It's a fair question. What shall I say if I *do* meet one of these nasty pirates?"

Beowulf listened intently as the unseen Frisian finally ran out of patience. Calling on his men to row on after the other boats he turned and snapped back.

"You can tell them that they had best hurry back to Dorestada if they want the chance to travel to valhall with their king. He dies tomorrow."

THIRTEEN

Hygelac walked up the gentle slope and planted the white boar flag of Geatland firmly into its highest point. Messengers were moving along the rear of the Geat shield wall relaying his orders to the weary warriors and, as he looked on in satisfaction from his vantage point, the line of men turned and jogged quickly across to reform on his new position in a jangle of mail and leather. His mind automatically parcelled up the groups as they passed him by and by his reckoning they had taken about five hundred casualties in the fighting so far, fully one quarter of his entire force. The trees to his rear were thick now with crows of all kinds and more of them were arriving all the time. High above the air was as thick as pottage with them and the king wondered how they could know that a battle was imminent.

A heavy *thwack* from the direction of the ballista drew his attention back to the river crossing and he watched with relief as the heavy bolt flew high and wide to the right of them. It was a ranging shot he knew and there would be others soon as, now shorn of the protection of the built up river bank, the Francs groped to find the correct combination of power and elevation on their monstrous contraptions. When they did the results would be ruinous for the reformed shield wall and the king searched desperately for the opportunity to make the attack he had formulated with his leading men earlier.

Another bolt whizzed over their heads, much closer this time, to embed itself in a tree to the rear with a solid *thunk* sending a thunderhead of crows cawing, panic stricken, into the sky. Tofi glanced at Hygelac as the men ducked involuntarily despite the fact that the bolt was clearly flying high and wide.

"They won't be able to stand against that, lord. Not once the bastards find the range."

Hygelac nodded grimly. He knew that the majority of the men in the army were farmers and freemen who owed service to their thegn. They had come here out of obligation and a chance for enrichment and could hardly be expected to face the power of the ballista.

"What do you think?"

Tofi peered down at the bolt throwing engine, still on the opposite bank, and, twisting around , up at the damaged trees. Looking back he pulled a wry smile.

"Only the far end of the shield wall is directly in line with them. If we shorten the line and swing around with the bridge to our rear we can help the boys there survive longer and give our defence greater depth." He shrugged. "It will be a tough nut to crack, lord."

Hygelac looked across and nodded.

"I think that we are going to get our nuts cracked soon enough whether we move or not, but its a good idea. Besides," he exclaimed gleefully, "it looks as if the Allfather may have been listening in on our plans earlier!"

Hygelac pointed down at the river crossing. A striking warrior dismounted and started to cross as a man carrying the francisca banner of the Francs scrambled to keep pace. Shielding their eyes against the glare of the lowering sun a huge grin slowly played across the features of the two Geats as they realised that the man and his retinue could only be a member of the Francish royal family and his retainers, maybe even King Theodoric himself. Hygelac punched Tofi delightedly on the arm.

"Get it done quickly and then get back. If we can tempt these boys to get close enough I am going to attack!"

The Francish warriors already on the Geat side of the river turned and roared their acclamation as the figure hopped across onto the bank. Immediately the Frisian leader dismounted and moved across to greet the newcomer and Hygelac noted with surprise that the pair seemed to be good friends. He had noticed that the Frisian fought under the banner of a black raven, Woden's bird, and he was surprised and disappointed to see the depth of affection which seemed to exist between the two leaders. Although the Francs had only abandoned the true gods for this White Christ several decades earlier, the vigour with which they had sought to convert their neighbours to the new god had become well known even in the far north.

Hygelac watched the men intensely as they parted, his eyes flicking from left to right as he watched the forces of the fiend jostle themselves into their own shield walls. The Frisians were now all but set in their position, one hundred yards away from the right wing of the Geat wall and he watched, hawk like, as the giant warrior with the raven wings attached to his helm swept from sight as he rode to the rear. The Geat leader, his heart thumping hard in his chest, looked back to the front and shielded his eyes as the sun, now a ball of orange flame, stood low to the West. Scores of men were still scrambling across the pontoon to join their king on the northern bank and a veritable flood of warriors were surging forward, crowding the southern bank as they attempted to cross.

To his delight Hygelac watched as the Francish line moved forward fifty paces and halted as they began to chant their war cries. As they did so the crow-wizards stepped forward to bless the warriors as he had expected them to do, inadvertently obscuring the ballista on the far bank and removing the very real threat to his plans which they had formed.

The sequence of events before him could only have been the work of the Allfather and Hygelac closed his eyes briefly and muttered a few words of gratitude to the war god. His decision made he turned to address his hearth warriors for what he knew would be the final time. Already privy to his plans he found that they had known that the decision had been made before he could open his mouth. Immediately to his rear Wulf and Tofi were embracing in a final display of friendship, whilst all around men were saying their final farewells to friends and kinsmen. A knot of emotion welled up in the king's throat as he witnessed the bravery on display in his army and he felt a strange mix of pride and regret that he should have led such men to their end. Wulf's arm reached out and drew his lord into the group, all deference to rank momentarily forgotten and for a fleeting moment the king knew the freedom and brotherhood of the hearth warrior for a final time. As they stepped back he remembered the last of their group, about to become the protector of a flank which was no longer there.

"Go and grab Thurgar and his boys, as quick as you can," he muttered to Tofi. "We go the moment you get back."

Hefting his shield Hygelac closed his hand around the throwing spear and tossed it as he sought the point of perfect balance. It was the same angon which he had used to kill the first of the Huns earlier that day and he knew that Woden would appreciate the gesture. Inhaling deeply Hygelac ran his gaze across the scene before him. The meadow sloped gently down, a drugget of daisies and buttercups. A smattering of white butterflies flitted from blossom to blossom as the warm winds of high summer swept them to and fro. Suddenly a gust swept one of them over to land on the rim of a warriors shield and Hygelac marvelled as the man removed it gently with his finger and ushered it on its way to safety. Faced with death any life became precious, he reflected sadly. A familiar deep voice boomed over his shoulder.

"We are here, lord, and I remembered to bring the cups for later," it joked. "Woden might be short of cups with the numbers of new guests he is about to receive!"

Hygelac turned and embraced the startled Thurgar as his friends pummelled his back, glad that their comitatus was complete again. Hygelac turned back and checked that all was still well.

To his right the Frisian leader, the raven man, had yet to reach the front rank of their shield wall. To the front the crow-wizards were still swinging smoky pots about on the end of a rope for some obscure reason and the Francish line was still far from complete. At its centre, directly ahead of him down the gentle incline stood the king of Francs surrounded by his banners and crosses. Now would be the time to start their barritus he knew, the great war cry of the northern folk, but he was also aware that this opportunity would pass in moments. Besides, he snorted gently, the power of the barritus would foretell the victor in the coming duel and that result was already known to each and every man standing on the field.

Hygelac flicked a look to left and right and was gratified to see that his gaze was returned by every man in the Geat army. All eyes were on him and him alone as they waited for the cry which would unleash their death charge.

Raising his shield and angon Hygelac roared out the name of their folk.

"Geats!"

As the answering roar from the army rolled down the slope the king bounded forward at the only place that a king of Geats should die, the very apex of a boiling, roistering boar snout.

*

Beowulf, Cola and Hrafn trotted their mounts towards the small group of men who were guarding the bridge. At their approach, one of the guards hopped down from the parapet and ambled into the road, holding up a hand to indicate that they rein in as he did so.

Beowulf flicked open the 'peace bands' which held his sword in place and did as he was bid, drawing to a halt several paces before the man. The other men had noticed the quality and bearing of the warriors who had appeared suddenly at the entrance to their bridge and slowly and self consciously lowered themselves to the roadway, straightening their leather jerkins as they did so. The first guard nodded slightly to his obvious superior and, almost apologetically, asked them to identify themselves. Beowulf smiled warmly and answered in his friendliest tone.

"My name is Beowulf Ecgtheowson, Ealdorman of Geatwic and these men are Cola, an Engle and Hrafn a Swede. We are on the way to rejoin our king at Dorestada. Are we still going in the right direction?"

Beowulf managed to keep a straight face as the guard's puzzled expression turned to horror as he realised that the appearance and accent of the warriors before him did indeed indicate that they were the enemy he had been told to guard the bridge against.

Beowulf reached his right hand across and drew his sword, Naegling, with a satisfying swish and examined the blade as Cola and Hrafn urged their mounts alongside his. He noticed that Cola was shaking his head sternly at the group of men on the bridge as their hands moved across to hover near the shafts of the spears which they had stacked haphazardly in a small recess. Beowulf examined the swirls and patterns made in the blade by the master smith centuries ago as they flashed and gleamed in the early afternoon sun. It really was a thing of exquisite beauty. He could, and had on occasion, marvelled at the workmanship all day but today he was in a hurry. Today he was going to war.

"I need an answer very quickly. If I had not had a question you would all be dead already so I would hurry if

I were you. Apparently there is going to be a big fight today and I want to be in it."

The guard looked quickly from Beowulf's sword, over to his companions and back to Neagling. It was obvious to him that he was on his own and any thoughts of resistance quickly melted away.

"I heard that too, lord," he eventually replied. He had apparently decided that he was about to die and would go with as much dignity as possible. Beowulf was impressed. He was at least a head taller than almost any man and powerfully built. He was also fully armed, a Geat lord dressed for war, and as such he was intended to intimidate by his presence alone. He decided that he would spare the man's life if he could. He raised his brow, indicating that the Franc continue with his answer.

"Yes, lord, this is the road. If you follow it down it will take you directly to Dorestada, as straight as a spear."

Beowulf nodded.

"How far is it?"

The guard pulled a face as he thought.

"Twenty, twenty-five miles or so, lord. There are the remains of an old Roman cavalry station at a place called Mannaricium which is about four or five miles short of the place. If you look out for the mile markers which they left beside the road they will count you down until you get there."

Beowulf nodded, satisfied.

"What is your name?"

"Childerich, lord."

Beowulf fished inside the purse which hung at his waist and tossed the astonished man a small gold coin.

"Here, Childerich, you have balls you deserve it. Now swallow it, it would be a shame to lose it so soon."

The guard looked at them in confusion.

"Lord?"

"Swallow it quickly and you can get it back in a few days time. Delay me any longer and I will take your head off here and now."

The Franc hastily swallowed the coin as his companions looked on, bemused.

"Right, all of you. Leave your weapons here, run to the middle of the bridge and jump in. Any man that I catch up with I will kill. Go quickly!"

After a heartbeat's indecision the Francs tore across the bridge and leapt over the parapet, landing moments later in a series of dull splashes far below. Cola dismounted and, scooping up the discarded weapons gave them a quick appraisal. After a moment he looked up at his lord and shook his head in disgust.

"Nothing worth having here, lord, it's all crap."

Beowulf nodded, he had suspected as much.

"Throw it downstream and let's get going. We have wasted long enough here but at least we now know that we are on the right road. We will be there in a few hours, let's go!"

*

They had left Bebba soon after the dawn had broken, red and menacing, on the eastern skyline. Beowulf had agreed with the Saxon boat master's view that it would be far too risky to travel to Dorestada along the Rin and they had berthed at a small trading settlement on the southern bank of the river an hour before dawn. They were close to the town of Arnheim and therefore firmly in the territory of the Francs but as with all border areas gold and silver ruled amongst the traders who inhabited these parts far more than the edicts of distant kings and lords.

Bebba had astonished Beowulf as he had slipped off the hammer of Thunor which he wore at his neck and replaced it with a symbol of the Christian nailed man but, as the trader had replied with a nonchalant shrug, "it enables me to trade and stay in these parts. A man has to make a living and after all," he laughed unashamedly, "there is no harm in adding another god to your collection is there! They all know that I keep a shrine to the gods at home in Saxland but they are happy to turn a blind eye and play along if there is a profit to be made. We are all not so different after all."

His point had been backed up by the immediate change in mood of the contact which Bebba had rousted from his bed in the iron-grey light of the pre-dawn. Good silver had exchanged hands and very soon they had been bidding a grateful farewell to the boat master and his delighted, if slightly dishevelled, trading partner as they rode west on three fine horses under the slowly lightening sky.

If they had thought that the journey back to the army would be as simple as following a road which ran 'as straight as a spear' they were soon to be cruelly disappointed. The lowlands hereabouts were crisscrossed with rivers and watercourses of all descriptions, from mighty rivers to rivulets and drainage ditches, and it became increasingly evident that every crossing place had been guarded by the enemy.

143

Usually it was only a few inexperienced warriors, not much more than armed townsmen, but it was obvious that they could not fight their way through each and every group without bringing more serious opposition to their progress down upon them. Everywhere they looked the tell tale sign of armed men on the move became increasingly evident. Dust clouds climbed into the hot summer sky and mid morning they had been forced to watch from afar as a large host passed to their front heading down from the north. The sea eagle banner which flew proudly above the leading elements clearly indicated that the army of the Fris had not been as comprehensively defeated earlier in the summer as they had been led to believe, a fact supported by the raven banner of Woden which snapped at its side.

Reluctantly Beowulf had had to turn away from the fine Roman Road and move to the North. By taking the byways which shadowed the main route he would arrive at the town later than he had hoped but at least he could be more certain that he would in fact reach his destination. They were three of the finest fighting men in the North but even they could not hope to fight their way through an entire army.

What was to have been a ride of a few short hours became a frustrating series of gallops and enforced halts as the enemy swirled around them like an incoming tide. Above them the cawing of crows filled the air as they hastened to the feast which men were about to provide for them and, glancing down to the South, Beowulf could tell the location of the town as a dark cloud of the birds washed to and fro above.

By late afternoon Beowulf, Cola and Hrafn were close enough to Dorestada to catch snippets of the sound of battle brought to them on the occasional gasps of wind, roars, cries and the familiar clash of steel on steel. Sporadically a sound which was unknown to them cut through the clamour as the *thwack* made by the gods knew what rent the air.

The track came up to a fine Roman Road which led directly south and, desperate now, Beowulf turned the head of his mount and took it. Ahead of him a slight rise led up to a town which could only be his destination and they kicked in and galloped alongside the Frisian stragglers. Wounded men moving to the rear told of the intensity of the fighting up ahead but the fact that the Fris had still obviously not broken and ran like he had expected them to gnawed at his mind. He had rushed to rejoin the army of his king and kinsman to share in the glory of a great victory but the first real seeds of doubt began to creep, unbidden and unwanted, into his being.

Approaching the lip of the rise Beowulf adjusted his helm strap and flicked open the peace bands which held Neagling secure in her scabbard. He had told Cola and Hrafn that he intended to gallop straight into the rear of the enemy force and cut a swath through to the Geat army before they could react. Any attack from an unexpected direction usually caused chaos among the lesser warriors who tended to congregate there. Before their leaders could react to the new threat he expected to be through the Fris line and safely back amongst his own people.

Taking up his shield he glanced to left and right as he checked that his men had moved up on him to form the wedge and was shocked to see a look of horror cross their

145

faces. Beowulf looked quickly back to the front and stared, dumbfounded, at the sight which greeted him.

FOURTEEN

Fifty yards, fifty paces, quickly became forty and then thirty as Hygelac tore across the grassy meadow like a rampaging bull. His senses sharpened as the battle fury came upon him and he became aware of the crashing of hundreds of booted feet and the metallic jangle of war gear even above the thunderous din of the Geat war cries. Ahead of him a few of the Francs, the more experienced old hands amongst them, were beginning to recover from their surprise and were hastily overlapping shields as the surge of northmen swept down on them. Hygelac realised that he was roaring maniacally as he saw the horror and panic etched onto their features. The front rank was going to form in time he could see, but the men to the rear still appeared to be finding their places. He still had a chance to punch through to the Francish leader but that chance would lessen by the moment.

At twenty paces Hygelac drew back his right arm and with a cry of dedication to the Allfather launched the angon over their heads, deep into the rear ranks of the fiend. Reaching across his body he drew his short stabbing seax with one smooth sweep and crashed on.

The king edged slightly to the right as a panic stricken crow-wizard finally realised the danger which was sweeping down on him and staggered comically backwards, dropping the strange smoking pot as he did so. Hygelac just managed to resisted the impulse to smash into the man as he knew that it would waste the energy of the charge and a heartbeat later he slammed into the Francs with a bone jarring crack as shield boss and linden board came together.

Hygelac gritted his teeth as he threw his left shoulder into the rear of the board and pushed desperately against the weight of the defenders. He caught his breath in alarm as his standing foot began to slip and slide on the damp ground, to lose your footing in this place meant almost immediate and certain death, but an instant later Thurgar's shield thumped into his back, lifting him forward and knocking the breath from his lungs in a painful rush. Suddenly he realised that Wulf and Tofi were on his flanks and they pushed forward together as the sounds of fighting spread along the entire front.

A face moved into his field of vision, the man's arm raised as he attempted to stab down with a short spear and Hygelac desperately tried to free his right arm and bring his seax up to parry the thrust but he was wedged tightly in the crush of bodies, unable to move. Grunting with the effort he redoubled his drive forward and was rewarded with the gain of a few extra inches. It was enough and the point of the framea glanced off of his helm and slid harmlessly down his side. The last push had opened up a small rift between the enemy shields before him and Hygelac worked his seax into the gap, pushing and probing until he felt the tip of his blade brush against the unmistakably metallic sensation of mail. With a sharp stab the blade tested the rings of steel and found them wanting. A scream of pain and horror arose from immediately to the king's front as his short sword burst through the links and slid easily into the soft organs behind them.

Hygelac risked a glance to the right as he drove forward and was gratified to see that his boar snout had punched deep inside the Francish shield burg. All along the line the Francs were wavering as the Geats hacked and pushed at them, driving themselves forward with all the ferocity of men whose sole aim was to gain the approval of their god, earning a place in his hall until they would accompany his war band at the end of days.

Hygelac surged forward a little more as further Geat warriors massed to the rear and added their weight to the push. A final duel was being enacted above him as framea darted back and forth and then, suddenly, he burst through the Francish line into clear space. The king opened his mouth to call to his hearth warriors but the familiar voice of Wulf cried above the din, anticipating the question.

"We are here, lord!"

A quick glance to left and right told the king that the line had been breached in several places and his men were streaming through. His standard bearer appeared at his side, panting with the exertion of the run and fight carrying the heavy *herebeacn,* the white boar of Geatland.

Hygelac's head snapped back to the front, sure that he was about to find the Francish forces tumbling away in disorder but to his dismay he found that he had only broken through the advanced ranks of the Francish position. A further fifty yards ahead of his now disordered troops, the enemy had drawn up in a solid wall of shields around their leader. Scores of spears were being added to the defence with every passing moment as more and more men scrambled across the pontoon from the southern bank.

As Hygelac hesitated a roar came from his right and he swung round just in time to see the *herebeacn* of the Fris carve its way deeply into the Geat flank, rolling up the line like a great steel and leather clad wave . Suddenly it was Geatish warriors who were scrambling, panic stricken, away from an aggressive and well led charge and Hygelac watched in dismay as the disaster unfolded.

It could be only a short while now until the end and his mind raced as he weighed up the rapidly diminishing options still before him. He glanced back at the Franc shield burg but instantly discounted a further attack. It was a further fifty paces away and his forces had lost all sense of cohesion in the assault on the forward position. Not only was it already too strong to attack but the defence was growing in numbers by the moment. He knew that great numbers of Francs would be streaming across the bridge which they had finally left undefended to the rear and an attack from that direction must be imminent. In truth there was only one place where they could hope to make any impression before they were wiped out and, as if to confirm his choice, the black and blue raven banner of the Frisian champion hove into view.

Hygelac turned to his remaining hearth warriors as he made to sheath his seax. To his embarrassment he could not find the mouth of the scabbard and he hoped that his men would not take it as a sign of nerves as he jabbed again and again at thin air but, to his surprise, he found that they were all laughing. Wulf nodded his head down as he explained.

"You seem to have mislaid it, lord."

Hygelac looked down and was shocked to see that a great gash had been opened up in the side of his mail shirt by what he imagined must have been a spear thrust. The weapon had carried on and removed both his purse and seax scabbard as it passed within a whisker of disembowelling him.

The king joined in the laughter and tossed the fabulously crafted blade to the ground.

All around him the last flickers of Geat resistance were dying down. Men stood in small groups, back to back, as they attempted to ward off the blows which now came at them from all sides in a desperate attempt to live a heartbeat longer.

The king turned to the grim faced warrior still resolutely holding the *herebeacn*. It was a position of high honour in the army to carry the white boar into battle and Hygelac nodded to the man in recognition of his bravery that day. After the king himself the man would have been the focal point of any attack by their fiend and he had done magnificently well to carry it to the end.

King Hygelac drew his sword and heft his battered shield for the last time on middle earth. Sweeping a last smile around his hearth warriors and closest friends he roared his battle cry and bolted towards the raven warrior.

*

Beowulf gasped at the scene which unfolded before him as he cleared the rise. In his worst nightmares he had thought to find the army of the Geats resolutely defending the town against a horde of Francs and Frisians, but in truth he had quickly dismissed even that scenario as ridiculous. The Saxons had all agreed that the Fris had been defeated at the start of the campaign and, although they had warned him of the size of the Francish army, they had themselves shown no great fear of it. They had clearly been accustomed to fighting and beating them on a regular basis and there was no reason to doubt that the Geats would not do likewise.

He looked across in stunned disbelief as he realised that he may be witnessing the heroic death of a great king.

Slowly his years of training reasserted themselves and he began to read the information which lay spread out before him. The town of Dorestada nestled against the banks of the river Rin. Ahead of him, straight down the road on which his horse stood patiently waiting for its next command, was a bridge which appeared to be held by a small Geat force and away to the right a pontoon bridge had been constructed from a number of boats. The crushed grass on the far bank told that a large number of men had crossed here, outflanking the men on the bridge and moving forward up the slight rise ahead. They were obviously the Fris and he could see them fighting now under their sea eagle banners. To the right of these a large force of Francs seemed to be watching the fight from a strong defensive position under their own Francisca flags and wooden crosses.

The fighting was all but over with small knots of men fighting to the last all over the field but he watched with a strange mixture of horror and unbelievable pride as the last organised group of Geats disappeared into the great wall of Fris. There was a brief struggle and then the white boar *herebeacn* of his people dipped, was thrust upwards for a final time into the golden light of the sunset before being beaten down into the shadows.

A tremendous roar of victory arose from the throats of thousands of men as they wildly celebrated both the demise of their enemy and the now almost certain fact that they themselves would live to see another day.

Beowulf became aware that Cola and Hrafn had walked their mounts forward to come abreast of him. Cola's voice cracked with emotion as he tore his gaze from the field opposite and looked at his lord.

"Shall we go, lord?"

Beowulf looked at him in confusion.

"Go? Go where?"

"Back to the coast, lord. The ships must be there with the rest of the army."

Beowulf swung round as he realised the importance of his hearth warrior's words.

"Of course!" he exclaimed as he broke into a relieved smile. "What was it that Brand said?"

Hrafn nodded as the words came back to him. Looking at the numbers of bodies strewn across the field before them there was no way that they represented the full contingent of warriors who had sailed south.

"The only way that the Francs will defeat your king is if he makes a mistake like dividing his forces," Hrafn repeated before they all chirped together, "which he would never do, would he lord!"

It was obvious to Beowulf now that the Francs and Frisians *had* caught them with their army divided. The absence of the ships indicated that a large part of the army had already left the town and either returned to the Aelmere or sailed directly downriver to the German Sea. A sudden thought gripped Beowulf like an icy fist. Hygelac would have commanded one force himself and appointed his son, Beowulf's cousin, Heardred, to lead the other. He had just watched one of them die in the meadow opposite but which one? Both were kinsmen, Hygelac his uncle and one time foster father and his cousin Heardred his closest friend. Without making a conscious decision he suddenly found that he had urged his mount on, into the town. The answer to his question lay there he knew and, although he dreaded the finality of knowing, he knew that he must.

Dorestada was a settlement built on two shallow but distinct terraces above the river, no doubt he reflected, as a result of the road and bridge which crossed the Rin at this point. From the sounds of the celebrations which were rolling across the town from the southern bank it was clear that the fighting was over and the population were beginning to cautiously venture from their homes again. A few began to join in the victory celebrations until the sound of horses caused them to turn and scatter as they recognised the Geats for what they were.

The echoing sound made by their hoof beats changed abruptly as they clattered down the final terrace and emerged onto a wide waterfront. Ahead of them a small force of Fris were too busy congratulating each other and hurling abuse at the isolated Geat force to notice their arrival and they simply steered their mounts through the gaps between the dancing men and clumped onto the bridge.

Dismounting, Beowulf strode forward to the warrior who had come forward to greet him and gratefully took the proffered ale barrel, gulping down the heady brew as Cola and Hrafn did likewise at his side. He finished with a gasp of pleasure and, wiping his beard on his sleeve, smiled at the man before him.

"Ealdorman Hromund, any news?"

A rumble of ironic laughter ran through the Geatish warriors at the absurdity of the question and Hromund shook his head wearily.

"Beowulf, why are you here? This fight took place before you arrived, there is no disgrace in not throwing your life away chasing a dead cause. Get back on your horse and get to the coast while you still have a chance!"

Beowulf shook his head.

"I watched a kinsman die from that rise, so I *was* here. Tell me who led our army so magnificently, I have a duty to avenge him."

Hromund pulled a wry smile and nodded that he understood. It was one of the most important obligations of kinship that a killing be compensated in blood or gold.

"My friend King Hygelac led the Geats here. Your cousin Heardred sailed for the German Sea two days ago. We were to make a last sweep along the Rin and meet up at the coast in a week and head home." He grimaced. "They could not have caught us at a worse time, Beowulf, divided and without our ships."

Beowulf took a final long draught from the barrel and swung himself back onto his mount. Cola and Hrafn followed suit and Beowulf made to tell them to stay with Hromund and his men before he recognised the futility. The time had come for every man to choose his place to die and he would not be the one to deny them the right to go to the Allfather having fulfilled their vows and fall at their lord's side.

Urging his mount forward with a click of his tongue, Beowulf walked the horse down to the body of Fris warriors guarding the southern end of the bridge. The men there had finally realised that mounted warriors had appeared on the bridge which they had been tasked with guarding and had stopped celebrating the victory on the meadow behind them and rushed back to their duty.

To Beowulf's amusement the man in charge of the group called his men together and formed two ranks in honour of the party in the mistaken assumption that they must be a Frisian lord and his hearth warriors. It was an understandable mistake. They *had* been distracted and they knew for a fact that the Geats on the bridge had no horses with them. The bearing and quality of their armour and weapons clearly marked them out as elite warriors, possibly royal, and he had reacted accordingly.

Beowulf kicked in and trotted through the ranks of Frisian warriors as Hromund's men, fortified by their attempts at denying the Fris any remaining ale as spoils of war, howled with laughter on the bridge. He glanced down at the leading Frisian and nodded his thanks, smiling at the confusion writ large on the man's face as the cries and catcalls from the watching Geats began to sow the first seeds of doubt in his mind. Breaking through, Beowulf urged his horse into a trot, angling off towards the cluster of banners midway across the slight slope, only slowing his mount into a walk as he became sure that he was out of spear range of the Fris. An angon in the back from an embarrassed guard would be an idiotic way to die after all they had been through to get here.

The first flush of victory was subsiding amongst the warriors as he reached the scene of the battle and they were beginning to hurry about in a desperate scramble to loot the bodies of the fallen Geats before others beat them to the choicest pickings. Beowulf reined in at the edge of the scene of fighting and studied the ground with a practised eye. Any warrior of his experience could read a battlefield as well as a wizard could read rune sticks and this was as clear as he had ever seen.

The king had almost been surprised by the arrival of the Francs and had rushed his main force forward to delay them at this river, leaving a small force under Hromund to guard their escape route as they either gathered in the horses or recalled the ships. Unfortunately the Frisians had arrived from the North and trapped them on this peninsula. After heavy fighting both Geat positions had been outflanked by river crossings and Hygelac had pulled his men back to the slight rise to the left. At bay and with no hope of relief, the king had chosen to attack the enemy and ensure his place at the benches of valhall rather than become overwhelmed where he stood at bay.

A ragged line of bloodied and gore covered bodies marked the point of contact of the opposing shield walls at the foot of the slope and a little further on numerous sad islands marked the last defensive positions taken up by the groups of Geats who managed to break through the Francish shield wall only to become cut off in the clearer space beyond.

Swirls of crows were circling the field like an angry cloud and the trees away to the left were a mass of cawing impatience as they waited for the bodies of the dead to be stripped and abandoned to their razor-like beaks.

Away to the West the horses had pulled the sun ever lower as the iron-grey wolf chased her down. The sky now was a brawl of reds and yellows as Beowulf raised his gaze, seeking out the standard of the Francs from the midst of the waving, jostling multitude.

Suddenly he saw it, the francisca banner of King Theodoric and his clan and he snorted at his inability to spot the largest banner on the field earlier. It was of course the only one stationary, kings do not wander over battlefields like overexcited women, men collect the spoils of war and bring them to him. He turned the head of his mount away from the death field and walked it across.

Dismounting nearby Beowulf, Cola and Hrafn unbound their shields and checked their equipment, tightening straps on war shirts, arm guards and helms. Beowulf ran his hand over the face of his shield and gazed on its beauty for what he imagined would be the last time, smiling as he remembered the moment that he had been presented with it. It had been a gift from his grandfather, King Hrethel, Hygelac's father, the moment he had passed the initiation ritual and been accepted into the brotherhood of the wolf warriors. That night he had been reborn as a man and it was fitting that the shield accompany him in death. He ran his hand across the gilt eagle and boar figures which adorned the face of the shield and recalled the fights with each which had caused them to be fashioned.

Looking up he realised that his men were waiting for him to lead them forward and he smiled and clasped them warmly to him. No words passed between them, none were needed, and they turned and, flicking the silk peace bands from the hilt of their swords, strode purposely towards the carousing Francs.

The king was standing beneath the royal banner, surrounded by a knot of magnificently attired warriors, obviously Francish lords and their hearth warriors, and as he drew closer he noticed with disdain that few of them seemed to have sullied their flamboyant armour that day. The king made a comment and the lords laughed heartily though not, he noted with approval the hearth warriors, who remained alert to any danger to their lord even at the moment of victory.

As they grew near one of the warriors smiled at a comment made by his friend and continued casually passing his gaze over the men nearby. Suddenly he must have realised that there was something out of the ordinary with the group of three warriors who were walking deliberately towards them. The smile fell from his face and his head snapped back as he brought his framea down and challenged them.

"Stay where you are and give me your names!"

Beowulf halted and planted his feet four square. He was close enough now for his voice to carry to the king and he waited until the group turned his way as warriors rushed to support their fellow sentinel. As the conversations trailed away Beowulf drew his sword and clashed the blade three times against the steel rim of his shield as he began the ritual challenge.

"Greetings to Theodoric, shield of the Francs.

I am Hygelac's kinsman, a member of his hall troop.

As a young man Woden, fury, granted me victories against both my king's fiend and hel's slathering monsters.

Beowulf Ecgtheowson is my name, Ealdorman of the Waegmundings, a Geatish folk.

Each man here knows the truth that it is better to avenge the slaying of dear ones then indulge in useless mourning.

Living in this world means waiting for our end for each of us.

Let every warrior here hope for an end such as the Allfather, Lord of Battle Play, gifted my kinsman here this day.

Whoever can do so let them win glory before death, a reputation to ring down the ages for as long as men huddle in smoky halls and regale each other with tales of heroes to chase away the dark winter nights.

I stand before you to demand the wergild for a slain kinsman as is the custom everywhere.

Send forth Hygelac's slayer that I may claim the blood-price for the loss of a great king."

A gentle ripple of laughter had run through the watching Francs as Beowulf had begun his address but it had quickly tailed away as they realised both the identity of the newcomer and the purpose of his challenge. The Francish lords turned to their leader as the warriors held Beowulf at spears length. Beowulf could see now that the Franc was a young man, younger than himself, and he realised that he must have misidentified him during the challenge. The man came forward and pushed his way through the cordon of spear men, dismissing the protestations of his lords with a casual flick of his hand. He nodded respectfully as Beowulf glared down at him.

"Beowulf Ecgtheowson, your reputation is known to me."

Nervous spear men were beginning to move to the flanks of Beowulf and his men as they sought to protect their lord from harm but the Franc glanced across and waved them away.

"Forgive my men from laughing during your challenge, they are still in high spirits. I am afraid that you assumed that I was my father, Theodoric. I am Theudobert, I commanded here."

Beowulf lowered his head in supplication.

"I apologise, lord. I have just arrived at this place."

To his surprise Theudobert chuckled.

"Yes, I know. You have spent the summer in Saxland so, if I am not mistaken, you have not so much as raised your voice against our people, much less a sword. Happily that means that I have no quarrel with you and you are free to leave."

Beowulf breathed deeply as he sought to compose himself.

"I did not come here to ask your permission to return home, lord. I owe a duty of honour to avenge the death of a kinsman, a man dear to me, my king."

Theudobert's expression hardened as he replied.

"You are in a Christian kingdom now Beowulf, your heathen feuding has no place here. The Lord of Hosts rules matters spiritual, he will dispense his wisdom to the slayer of Hygelac on the day of judgement as he will us all. I advise you to leave now whilst you are still able."

The change in tone had not gone unnoticed and Cola and Hrafn moved forward to flank their lord. Immediately the Francish warriors moved in and raised their spears threateningly at the Geats.

Suddenly another voice broke in, a voice dripping with undisguised menace.

"Then it is fortunate that I still honour Woden, lord. I killed the pirate king and I relish the chance to send another Swerting journeying across the rainbow bridge!"

Beowulf tensed as a powerful warrior pushed through the ranks of spear men flanked by two of his own hearth warriors. Scarcely shorter than Beowulf, the man looked imposing in highly polished mail and greaves. A helm of polished steel was quartered by a magnificent gilt rendering of a raven in flight and from the very apex of the helm, lifting and falling gently in the late evening breeze, there hung a pair of the dark splayed wings of Woden's bird. A curtain of mail hung suspended from the lower edge of the helm, its metallic swish adding greatly to the feeling of power and menace which the warrior projected. He nodded to Beowulf and continued.

"I am Dayraven of the Hugas, A Frisian folk. Your king and his people thought us weak but he was mistaken. Now he sups with the others of your foul clan in Woden's hall. Soon you will join them, Beowulf. Save me a place at the benches for when I follow on."

Beowulf answered.

"The time for idle boasts is past, Dayraven of the Hugas, killer of old men. Will you fight me within the hazel or will you wait until your Christian overlords rush to save you again? A summer spent hiding in your marshes seems to have addled your mind. I have no desire for compensation, it is a blood price which I demand!"

Dayraven stiffened at the insult and indicated to one of his men with a flick of his head.

"Get down to the river and bring the hazel. Let us finish this."

*

The light was fading quickly as Dayraven's hearth warrior returned with the hazel rods. Cola helped the man to mark out the holm gang, the island way, on which the duel would take place. It was the custom in the North that ritual challenges be fought to the death on an island, well away from any sources of aid or easy escape, but often the fighting area was marked out as a space nine paces square, each corner marked by a hazel withy. Nine represented the number of nights which the Allfather had hung on the world tree as he had sought to gain the knowledge of the runes and the fight would be dedicated to Woden and fought in his honour.

A ring of torches were placed around the square and Theudobert and the senior Francs took up their places as the lesser warriors of Francland and Frisia jostled for the best positions at the remaining three sides.

Beowulf cast off his thick leather battle shirt and discarded his heavy mail byrnie. A dew was beginning to form on the surface of the grass as it cooled after the heat of the day and he knew that the surface of the holm gang would quickly become treacherous. A great cheer rent the air and Beowulf glanced across to see that his opponent had crossed the line which marked the holm gang. Once Beowulf crossed that line only one of them could emerge alive.

To his surprise Beowulf saw that Dayraven had remained in his full armour complete with the heavy helm which he had worn earlier. His heart leapt at the stupidity of his opponent and he had to force himself to remain calm and not allow himself to underestimate his foe as he hurriedly changed his tactics. The holm gang was no place for heavy armour and full faced grim helm. A warrior needed steel and weight and power in the shield wall, strength to push and harry as men grappled as close as lovers. In the confined space of the holm gang, Beowulf knew, you need to be sharp and swift in mind and body and he found himself wondering if this Dayraven had ever taken the island way.

He glanced back at the Frisian who stood at the opposite end of the square, beating his sword against his shield rim and urging his supporters into a frenzy. Beowulf turned back to his companions and laughed at their pinched expressions. They looked at him questioningly and he winked as he slipped off his under shirt and heft his shield. Drawing Neagling with a satisfying swish he handed the scabbard to Hrafn. Cola stepped forward and ensured that his helm was secure and then, with a final nod, Beowulf turned and crossed the line.

The Geat and the Frisian stood and regarded one another for a moment and, although he had instinctively checked on their first meeting, Beowulf found that he was searching the decorative plates which made up the dome of his opponents helm. To his satisfaction he was reassured that the dancing warrior design of the wolf warrior brotherhood was absent and he rolled his shoulders and neck muscles as he prepared for the contest.

The ritual dance which formed part of the initiation ceremony for new members of the brotherhood was far more than a meaningless series of gyrations he knew. The body movements which were incorporated within the dance consisted of a series of attacks and feints which would be invaluable in a contest such as the one he was about enter.

Suddenly Dayraven let out a tremendous roar and tore across the grass. Already expecting such an opening move from the big Frisian Beowulf skipped adroitly to one side as he thundered past. The watching warriors of the combined army screamed and gestured at the apparent timidity of the Geat, their faces thrown into grotesque masks of hate by the light from the flickering torches.

Dayraven recovered and moved forward, his heavy broadsword arcing through the warm summer air as he tried to corner his lightly armoured opponent. Beowulf skipped nimbly backwards, being careful to keep just ahead of the onslaught. All around him the taunts and cries of the allied warriors rose to a crescendo as Beowulf skilfully denied them the slogging match which they had obviously come to see.

The big Frisian hesitated and Beowulf knew that he must attack and force the man to keep moving. If he slowed down and started to think about his tactics it could ruin everything. With the suddenness of an adder strike Neagling flicked out. Taken unawares Dayraven was caught unbalanced and Beowulf's blade shot forward to slide between the man's shield rim and inner thigh. Beowulf saw his opponents eyes widen in shock and pain as the razor sharp edge sliced deeply into the muscle and tissue of his leg. Staggering backwards, Dayraven glanced down and Beowulf caught the look of surprise and horror as he saw that the legs of his trews were already dark with blood. They both knew that he had taken a bad wound and that he would quickly weaken. The weight of his armour would quickly begin to sap at his strength and Beowulf stepped back and awaited the inevitable onslaught as his opponent tried to end the contest as quickly as possible.

Something red and white began to dance in his peripheral vision and the crowd screamed with laughter and pointed at him to look. Beowulf glanced back at Dayraven and saw to his surprise that the Frisian appeared to look downcast as he prepared to attack again. Unable to look away Beowulf concentrated on the imminent attack. The nightmare that it could have been the bodies of Cola and Hrafn flashed into his mind and he frantically pushed the thought aside as Dayraven came on, screaming his war cry.

Beowulf was moving freely now as the sword-peace of an experienced warrior returned to him. Tired and now badly injured, Dayraven appeared to move at an almost serene pace. Unbalanced by the wound the Frisian's swing was poor and Beowulf easily danced inside the wild stroke. With a backward flick which was almost casual in its execution Beowulf sliced Neagling across and through the tendons at the back of Dayraven's knee. The big Frisian collapsed to the grass, his shield and sword spinning across into the line of flaring brands.

Safe from attack Beowulf could look across beyond the line of torches to the dancing thing and a cry caught in his throat as he realised that it was the disembowelled torso of his king. Hygelac's legs and arms had been hacked off above the knees and elbows and the hollow cavity of his body glistened with pale bone and bloody gore in the flickering lights of the torches. In a final moment of horror he saw that the Frisians had emasculated his kinsman and his genitals had been stuffed roughly into his mouth. Beowulf found that he was walking forward, towards the macabre sight, his sword raised and ready to strike, until Cola's cry from his right brought his attention crashing back to the duel.

Dayraven had struggled to his feet and was within a whisker of bringing his sword within range. The Geat danced back as his mind snapped back to the contest. Hygelac's killer was here and at his mercy and a primeval roar escaped from Beowulf as he parried the lame sword thrust of his opponent with ease. Moving forward he drove the sole of his boot forward into the man's undamaged knee. With a crack which reverberated around the meadow the knee joint burst asunder as Dayraven was sent flying backwards with a scream of pain.

Beowulf looked back across to the body of Hygelac but found to his disappointment that both it and his tormentor had gone. Walking across to Cola he handed his hearth warrior his sword and turned back to the prone figure of the Frisian champion.

Dayraven lay panting with pain as Beowulf crouched beside him. Reaching forward he brutally snapped the fastening of the grim helm and tore it from him. Hurling it contemptuously aside, Beowulf stared down with hate filled eyes and slowly and deliberately asked him the question.

"Were you the man who gutted my kinsman?"

The Frisian wanted to deny that he would do such a thing but his code of honour forbade him. The men who served him were his responsibility and acted in his name. He would have to accept the consequences of their actions and he lowered his gaze in shame.

With a grunt of rage Beowulf tore at Dayraven's mail shirt. One of the first things that Hygelac had worked on when he had taken Beowulf home to foster had been to strengthen the boy's grip and it was said that he now had the strength of thirty men in his grasp. Unequal to the attack, the links of Dayraven's mail burst open under the strain as Beowulf's fist beat on the man's breast with all of his might. Dayraven's ribcage broke with a sickening crack and Beowulf reached inside and tore the still beating heart from the Frisian's body. To the mounting horror of the watching Theudobert and his men, the heartless thing which Dayraven had now become managed to drag itself across to the place where its sword lay. With a final, superhuman effort, the hand of the Frisian warrior reached out and grasped the hilt one last time as it finally slumped down and grew still.

As a shocked silence descended over the field Beowulf stood and tossed the gory organ of his foe contemptuously aside.

He looked across the mutilated corpse of Dayraven and called to his hearth warriors.

"Cola...Hrafn; *Now* we can go."

AUTHOR NOTE

This novella was a result of my research into the great Anglo Saxon epic which is *Beowulf* for my Sword of Woden trilogy of novels. Although my novels ended with Beowulf's victories over Grendel and his mother, the descriptions of the event which is commonly referred to as 'Hygelac's Raid' seemed to cry out for a short story from amongst the seemingly interminable accounts of the wars between the Geats and Swedes for the control of what is now southern Sweden.

Amidst the shadowy conflicts which are alluded to in the poem the only historically identifiable event which occurred was the raid by the army of King Hygelac on the region we now know as the low countries. The raid was obviously a major event which was recorded in four independent sources, two Frankish and two Anglo Saxon, one of which was of course the Beowulf poem.

Of the existing sources the Frankish are naturally the most detailed and, although they call the invaders Danes in much the same way as the later Anglo Saxon Chronicle tended to refer to all later raiders in the same manner whatever their origins, there is no doubt that it is the same raid mentioned in Beowulf. Both the 'Historiarum Libri X' of Gregory of Tours and the slightly later 'Liber Historiæ Franconum' describe how the raiders, after a successful summer spent looting the lands of the Frisians and their southern neighbours the Hetware, were overtaken by a Frankish army under the king's son Theudobert after they had divided their army, presumably as a prelude to sailing home. King Hygelac was trapped and killed, and the Geat forces which remained with him ashore annihilated. The Frankish chronicles then go on to tell that the fleet was intercepted, probably at the mouth of the River Lek or the old, more northern, mouth of the River Rhine, and thoroughly defeated in a sea battle.

The raid is mentioned four times in the Beowulf story which describe the death of Hygelac with a large part of the Geat army and Beowulf's boast how he '...killed Dayraven the Frank in front of the two armies...' As to the manner of Beowulf's final victory I based the holm gang fight on the passage in the poem, 'It was not my sword that broke his bone cage and the beatings of his heart but my warlike hand grasp.' In addition to the four passages in Beowulf another East Anglian source, the 'Book of Monsters of Various Kinds' written around the year 800 mentions the fact that the giant bones of King Hygelac can still be seen on an island in the Rhine.

Although there is no agreement as to the exact year in which the raid occurred the general consensus seems to narrow it down to the period between 521 and 523 and I have chosen the summer months of the latter as it would tie in to the dating in the earlier books.

Rather than describe one long account of rape and pillage I decided to reintroduce the character of the

Danish warloca Unferth from the previous books. It allowed me to broaden the geographical scope to include the lands of the Saxons, but also added another layer to the tale.

If you enjoyed my Sword of Woden series you may be interested to know that the story of early sixth century Europe continues in my later series, King's Bane. Book one, Fire & Steel, is the first in a series of books which will tell the tale of the migration of the English people from their ancestral home in continental Angeln to the new lands in what came to be called England. Eofer, the king's bane of the title, is the Angle married to Hygelac's daughter Astrid in Sorrow Hill, the same man who killed King Ongentheow of the Swedes at the battle of Ravenswood in book three, Monsters.

There were many events which are alluded to within the Beowulf poem which fall outside the timeline of this series. Eofer king's bane, the new hero of our story, will carry his sword across the northern lands as he fights on behalf of both his own king and people and his Geatish kinsmen as our story continues.

Cliff May
February 2014.

CHARACTERS

ALBRUNA – A Saxon volur, a holy woman.
ALDWULF – Saxon Ealdorling of Honovere.
BEBBA – Saxon boatmaster.
BEOWULF – Geatish hero.
BJORN – Geat warrior at Dorestada.
BRAND – Saxon guide at the Osning.
COLA – Beowulf's English hearth warrior.
DAYRAVEN – Frisian hero.
EADRED – Saxon thegn near Theotmalli.
EALHSTAN – Hygelac's hearth warrior.
EINAR HAROLDSON – Geat scout.
FLOSI – Geat cook at Dorestada.
GEWIS – Saxon Ealdorling of Biranum.
GODWIN – Saxon hall steward at Honovere.
GUNNAR – Beowulf's hearth warrior.
HEARDRED – Son of Hygelac, Beowulf's cousin.
HJALTI – Geat guard at Dorestada.
HRAFN – Beowulf's Swedish hearth warrior.
HROMUND – Ealdorman of Geatwic.
HYGELAC – King of Geatland.
IDA – King of Frisland.

ING – A god.
KARI – Geat scout.
OFFA – An English scout.
OSLAF – An English scout.
SÆFUGOL – Sea Bird, Saxon thegn at Feddersen.
SAXNOT – Chief god the the Saxons.
SEAXWINE – Young Saxon guard at Feddersen.
THEUDOBERT – Son of Theodoric, leads the Francish army at Dorestada.
THEODORIC – King of Francs.
THUNOR – Son of Woden. A god.
THURGAR – Hygelac's hearth warrior.
TIWAZ – A god.
TOFI – Hygelac's hearth warrior.
ULF – Geat warrior at Dorestada.
UNFERTH – Danish warloca.
WALDHERE – A Saxon thegn.
WILFRID – Saxon reeve at Biranum.
WODEN – The Allfather. A god.
WULF – Hygelac's hearth warrior.

PLACES/LOCATIONS

RIVER AELDU – River Alde, Suffolk, England.

THE AELMERE – The Ijsselmeer, Netherlands.

RIVER ALBIA – River Elbe, Germany.

RIVER ALERA – River Aller, Germany.

ARNHEIM – Eagle Home, Arnhem, Gelderland, Netherlands.

BIRANUM – Bremen, Niedersachsen, Germany.

DOMBURG – Walcheren, Netherlands.

DORESTADA – Near Wijk bij Duurstede, Utrecht, Netherlands.

RIVER EMESA – River Ems, Germany.

FEDDERSEN – Feddersen Wierde archaeological site, Niedersachsen, Germany.

FRANCLAND – France.

FRISLAND – Frisia, Netherlands.

FRIS TUN – Friston, Suffolk, England.

GEATLAND – South west Sweden.

HAMA BURG – Hamburg, Niedersachsen, Germany.

HEILIGEN LOH – Near Hoya, Niedersachsen, Germany.

HONOVERE – Hanover, Niedersachsen, Germany.

THE HUSEM – Nordfriesische inseln, Schleswig-Holstein, Germany.

IRMINSUL – The Externsteine, Nordrheine-Westfalen, Germany.

RIVER ISLA – Issel/Oude Ijssel, Germany/Netherlands.

RIVER LEINA – River Leine, Germany.

RIVER LUPIA – River Lippe, Germany.

MARKLO – Hoya, Niedersachsen, Germany.

RIVER MASA – River Maas/Meuse.

ANGLIA – East Anglia, England.

NOREGR – The North Way, Modern Norway.

OSNING – Teutoberger Wald, Germany.

RENDIL'S HAM – Rendlesham, Suffolk, England.

RIVER RIN – The Flowing One, River Rhine.

SAIMUND'S HAM – Saxmundham, Suffolk, England.

SANTEN – Xanten, Nordrheine-Westfalen, Germany.

SAXLAND – North West Germany.

RIVER SCEALD – The Shallow River - The Scheldt.

SNÆP – Snape, Suffolk, England.

THEOTMALLI – Detmold, Nordrheine-Westfalen, Germany.

TRONDELAG – Trondheim, Norway.

THE VECHT – An old course of the River Rhine.

RIVER WISERA – River Weser, Germany.

RIVER WOH – The Crooked River, River Waal.

ABOUT THE AUTHOR

Born in London and raised in Essex, I now live with my family on the Suffolk coast.

Visit my website at www.cliffordmay.com

30105466R00109

Printed in Great Britain
by Amazon